THE CROOKED BANISTER

Nancy and her friends Bess and George spend an exciting week exploring a mysterious zigzag house with its fantastically crooked staircase, its bizarre serpent picture, and an unpredictable robot that nearly causes the young detective to lose her life. But despite the threat of danger from the robot, Nancy is determined to solve the mystery of the weird house and to locate the missing owner, who is wanted by the police.

It takes keen logic and quick thinking for the young detective to plow through the tangled thicket of clues and find the key to this complex puzzle. With the help of her friends, Nancy captures an elusive swindler and uncovers the secret of the crooked banister, but not before they have several hair-raising adventures—one on a broken bridge over flaming water, another in a hidden room with poisoned portraits!

"The water's on fire!" Nancy exclaimed

NANCY DREW MYSTERY STORIES

The Crooked Banister

BY CAROLYN KEENE

PUBLISHERS *Grosset & Dunlap* NEW YORK

A NATIONAL GENERAL COMPANY

PUBLISHED SIMULTANEOUSLY IN CANADA

LIBRARY OF CONGRESS CATALOG CARD
NUMBER: 77-130336
ISBN 0-448-09548-3

PRINTED IN THE UNITED STATES OF AMERICA

Contents

The Crooked Banister

CHAPTER I

The Zigzag House

"Do you have any plans for the next few days, Nancy?" Carson Drew asked his daughter as she walked into their living room.

"No, not especially," the attractive girl replied. Smoothing back her reddish-blond hair, she sat down beside him on the long sofa. She added eagerly, "Dad, is there something I can do for you—for instance, solve a mystery?"

Mr. Drew, tall, handsome, and a leading attorney in River Heights, chuckled. "In a way, it is a mystery. Mr. and Mrs. Melody who live in town have been swindled by a Mountainville man named Rawley Banister. They want me to drive up there and put in a claim against him. I understand he was arrested on a similar charge."

"Is he in jail?" Nancy inquired.

Her father shook his head. "He's out on bail."

"Dad, you hinted that I might help you for the

next few days. I take it you plan to stay in Mountainville."

"Correct. I wanted Mr. and Mrs. Melody to accompany me, but he can't get away at this time."

Nancy's mouth puckered teasingly and her eyes twinkled. "Mrs. Melody is going, though, and you want me to make a threesome."

Mr. Drew grinned and said, "I thought you'd be interested in seeing Rawley Banister's fantastic home. He designed the house himself."

"What's fantastic about it?" Nancy asked.

"I guess just about everything. The house is on a wooded hilltop surrounded by a moat."

"Like a castle?" Nancy commented.

Mr. Drew nodded. "People around there say the water in the moat sometimes catches fire!"

Nancy gave her father a hug. "I can hardly wait to start. When do you want to go?"

"Tomorrow morning directly after breakfast."

"That doesn't leave me much time to decide what clothes to take," Nancy remarked.

She hurried upstairs to her bedroom and packed some summer knits. When the suitcase was filled, she went to the kitchen to help the Drews' housekeeper prepare supper.

Hannah Gruen was a lovable woman who had lived with Nancy and her father since the death of Mrs. Drew when Nancy was only three years old.

As the young detective walked into the kitchen, Mrs. Gruen said, "Your father mentioned you two are taking a trip. Do be careful, my dear. You always start out solving mysteries with the idea you'll be perfectly safe and you always end up getting into hot water."

Nancy smiled. How true Hannah's statement was! She said, "I'll be as careful as possible." Then she told the housekeeper why they were going.

"A swindler, eh?" Mrs. Gruen remarked. "The world is full of them and they always get caught in the end. Why do they do such things?"

Nancy did not comment. She agreed but was thinking that if there were no swindlers, there would be fewer mysteries for her to solve!

The following morning Nancy and her father set off in her convertible. Mr. Drew drove to Mrs. Melody's home and strode quickly up the front walk to carry down the woman's suitcase. She was in her early forties, and very pretty.

Mr. Drew introduced her and suggested that she and Nancy sit in the rear seat. "Mrs. Melody, will you explain to my daughter how you were swindled?"

Mrs. Melody said that a good-looking man who called himself George Ryder had sold the Melodys a piece of land in Arizona. It had turned out to be on an Indian reservation!

"Foolishly we had only looked at maps the

man had and fancy booklets showing beautiful homes surrounded by lovely bushes and flowers. Later my husband had business in Flagstaff and went to see our new piece of property. It was then that he discovered the swindle."

Nancy was puzzled. "You said the man's name was George Ryder. I thought the one who sold you the land was Rawley Banister."

"Actually you're right. When my husband tried to locate this George Ryder, he found the man had vanished. Just recently I happened to pick up the local newspaper and there was his picture. Only his real name was Rawley Banister and he'd been arrested."

Nancy remarked that he was out on bail.

"True," Mrs. Melody replied. "That's why your father and I thought we would go directly to the man's home in Mountainville, which had been mentioned in the article. We'll confront him with the fake deed, giving us title to the land."

Mr. Drew added, "And put in a claim at once for the Melodys to get back their money."

Two hours later they drove into Mountainville, a pleasant tree-shaded village with smart-looking shops and a motel. Mr. Drew stopped to ask a traffic policeman directions to the Rawley Banister house. The officer looked surprised but without comment gave the information.

After riding along streets lined with attractive

homes, Mr. Drew turned into a hilly driveway marked PRIVATE and started up the steep slope. Woods on both sides of the road completely concealed the house, until they were within a thousand feet of it.

"What a crazy-looking and scary place!" Mrs. Melody exclaimed.

Nancy added, "It's a real zigzag house."

The large building was made of fieldstone and lacked symmetry. Several walls had ugly protrusions, other walls were at a slant. Rising above the two stories were three slanting chimneys and a center tower with a windowed turret.

Beyond the parking area was a moat. The callers got out of the car and walked across a narrow steel bridge that had no railings. Between the moat and the building was a poorly kept lawn and a few bushes, all of them in grotesque shapes of unbalanced geometric figures.

"I wonder if the inside is as kooky as the outside," Mrs. Melody said.

The three walked up to the massive wooden front door, which had a large tarnished knocker but no bell. Mr. Drew lifted the knocker.

Almost at once a voice from inside said, "Mr. Banister is not at home. Come back some other time." The message was repeated and Nancy figured it was a recording.

"I guess we'll have to do as we were told," Mr. Drew said, grinning.

As the disappointed callers walked across the bridge, Nancy gazed down into the water and wondered if the story about it being on fire at times was a myth.

"But such a phenomenon would certainly fit this strange place," she thought.

When they returned to town Mr. Drew pulled into the grounds of the Ruppert Motel and went inside to inquire about rooms. A few minutes later a boy escorted them up an outside stairway to a balcony. The three rooms assigned to them were in the center and overlooked the parking area.

"I'll meet you two in the lobby," Mr. Drew said. "I have an errand to do."

Nancy and Mrs. Melody partially unpacked, then went downstairs together. They walked around the motel which was surrounded by artistic flower beds. By the time they reached the lobby, Mr. Drew was there. At once Nancy detected a worried look on his face.

"Dad, is anything the matter?" she asked.

Her father nodded. "I've just been talking to the desk clerk. He tells me that Rawley Banister has jumped bail and disappeared!"

"What!" Mrs. Melody cried in dismay. "Then our trip has been in vain?"

"Perhaps not," the lawyer replied. "The clerk told me that Rawley has a sister in town named

"What a crazy-looking place!" Mrs. Melody exclaimed

Mrs. Carrier. She lives in the old family homestead."

"Do you think she knows where her brother is?" Nancy queried.

"I doubt it," Mr. Drew replied. "Furthermore, Mrs. Carrier and another brother named Thomas put up the bail money!"

"How dreadful for them!" Mrs. Melody exclaimed.

Mr. Drew continued, "I think we'd better have some lunch. It's nearly two-thirty and that's when the dining room closes."

There was little conversation during the meal. All were disappointed by the turn of events. They figured that before Rawley Banister vanished, he had set the tape recorder to announce he was not at home.

"Do you think we can ever get inside the house?" Nancy asked.

"I hope so," her father answered. "We might pick up a clue there to his whereabouts."

Mr. Drew telephoned Mrs. Carrier. After hearing the story, she suggested that the trio come to her home that evening. "I prefer not to discuss my brother and his affairs on the telephone," she said.

"Of course," Mr. Drew replied. "Is eight o'clock a good time?"

"That will be fine."

Promptly at eight Mrs. Melody and the Drews

reached the Carrier home. A short, rather stout, sweet-faced woman opened the front door. She invited them in, and then to the surprise of the Drews, cried out, "Joyce Johnson!"

At the same moment Mrs. Melody exclaimed, "Sally Banister! I never connected you with Rawley Banister!" The two women embraced.

"No wonder. We always called him Jack."

Mrs. Melody turned to the Drews and introduced them to her boarding school classmate of years ago. "We'd completely lost track of each other."

Mrs. Carrier graciously acknowledged the introduction, then said a bit sadly, "I'm sorry Joyce and I have met again under such adverse circumstances. But do come in and we'll talk."

The Drews had been afraid Mrs. Carrier would be very guarded in her remarks and they would find out little. But now, learning that her schoolmate was a client of Mr. Drew, she talked freely.

"Rawley has always been a problem to our family," she told them. "Time and time again we helped him out of scrapes. Finally the police caught up with him and he was arrested on a swindling charge. As you already know, my brother Thomas and I put up bail and now we'll lose all that money. But this did not keep Rawley from disappearing. We have no idea where he is."

Mrs. Carrier went on to say that she had a feeling her brother did not intend to come back.

"He mailed me a note and a key to his front door. None of the family has ever been inside the place. We were never invited."

Nancy asked, "Were the contents of the note something you don't wish to reveal?"

"Oh not at all," Mrs. Carrier answered. "Rawley said, 'I dare you to find the Crooked Banister. Sorry I disgraced the family. You are now in charge of everything.' "

"The Crooked Banister?" Nancy queried.

Mrs. Carrier gave a wan smile. "My brother used to refer to himself as the Crooked Banister. And each time he said it, he would laugh. The rest of us didn't think it was funny."

She told Mrs. Melody, "Thomas and I will certainly repay you for every penny you lost."

Before Mrs. Melody could object, her friend changed the subject and said, "Would you people like to go out to Rawley's house tomorrow morning?"

"Oh yes," Nancy replied.

It was arranged that they would call for Mrs. Carrier about ten o'clock. Then, seeing that their hostess looked weary, the visitors left.

On the way back to the motel, they heard fire sirens. When they reached the Ruppert Motel all were astonished by what they saw.

"The motel's on fire!" Mrs. Melody cried out. "The smoke seems to be coming from our rooms!"

As they turned into the grounds, the police stopped them. Mr. Drew explained that they were staying there and he believed the fire was in their rooms.

"Sorry, but you can't go any farther!" a police officer said firmly.

The firemen had dragged long hoses up the balcony stairs and inside the bedrooms. It seemed strange to Nancy that all three rooms should be on fire at once and that none of the adjacent ones were. It was soon evident that the contents were either burned or water-soaked.

"I'm afraid everything is ruined!" Nancy said woefully.

"What's worse," her father added, "the copies of the deed and other papers to prove our claim against Rawley Banister were in my brief case!"

Mrs. Melody gasped. "And the originals were in my luggage!"

CHAPTER II

The Robot

"MAYBE we can save the papers!" Nancy burst out.

She rushed up to one of the firemen and asked if he could possibly retrieve the luggage. He shook his head. "Not a chance of its being any good. But the fire is out. I'll ask the chief if you can go to your rooms."

He called up to the balcony and repeated Nancy's request. The chief looked down.

"It's safe enough now. But there's a lot of water damage."

Mrs. Melody and the Drews hastened up the stairway. First they came to Mr. Drew's room.

He looked inside and exclaimed, "My brief case is gone!"

"How terrible!" Nancy said.

Mrs. Melody hurried along the balcony while Nancy stepped into her bedroom. Nothing seemed to be missing, but her suitcase was wide open. Every bit of clothing in it was soaked, as well as the dresses hanging in an alcove.

"What a mess this is!" she murmured.

The next moment she heard Mrs. Melody coming back. In an excited voice the woman said, "The papers concerning the property are missing! They must have been stolen!"

The fire chief looked at the three visitors quizzically, then called over a police inspector. "I suspected this incident was an incendiary act. Now these people say certain belongings of theirs have been stolen. There's no doubt in my mind but that the thief set the three blazes."

The Drews exchanged questioning glances. A suspicion was forming in their minds.

The inspector asked, "Have you folks any particular enemies?"

"Not that we know of," Mr. Drew replied, "but the stolen papers related to a case on which I'm working."

"My father is a lawyer," Nancy added.

The inspector made no further inquiries, but he wrote down Mr. Drew's name and address in case he wanted to get in touch with him. After the firemen had left and the motel manager had assigned Nancy, her father, and Mrs. Melody to rooms in another section, the three went to the lobby and sat down to discuss what had happened.

"I hate to say this," Mrs. Melody spoke up,

"but I suspect Rawley Banister was the one who stole the papers and set the fires."

Nancy agreed, but her father pointed out, "There's a possibility it could have been a confederate of his."

Mrs. Melody, suddenly realizing her night clothes had been burned, said she wondered if any shops in the motel or in town might still be open. Nancy asked the desk clerk and learned that a small department store up the street did not close until twelve. Since the most popular section of the shop was the soda counter which was filled with young people, the Drews assumed that was the main reason for its being open late.

The trio were able to purchase necessities to tide them over the night. In the morning they could buy other articles.

When they returned to the motel, Mrs. Melody said she was going to bed at once. Nancy asked her father to accompany her to the burned-out rooms.

"Maybe we can pick up a clue," Nancy added.

When they reached Mr. Drew's former room, they found a police detective at work there. He said he had located a number of fingerprints but doubted that any of them belonged to the burglar.

The Drews did not find a clue, either, in any of the rooms and walked onto the balcony. As Nancy stood looking out over the parking area, her foot touched something on the floor. Glancing down, she saw an unburned taper match in a crack and picked it up.

Nancy showed the long match to her father. "I'll bet the man who set the fires used one of these."

"It's a good guess."

Nancy went on, "When we go to Rawley Banister's house, I'll hunt for taper matches. If I find any like this one, it should be pretty good proof that it was Rawley who was here."

She could hardly wait for the next day to come. Now that the Drews were directly involved in the mystery, Nancy was eager to start work.

Although only eighteen, she had earned a reputation as an amateur detective by solving several cases, among them *The Secret of the Old Clock, The Hidden Staircase,* and most recently *The Mysterious Mannequin.*

The following morning when the Drews and Mrs. Melody arrived at Mrs. Carrier's home, they found her pale and nervous. Through a friend who was a newspaper reporter she had heard of the fires at the motel and the theft of important papers.

"I was sure they were yours and I'm terribly sorry. I know you must suspect, as I do, that the arsonist was my brother Rawley. Oh, it's dreadful to have a member of one's family do disgraceful things!"

She looked pleadingly at Nancy and her father. "The police have no trace of Rawley. Will you help me find him? I'm so worried that he's using an assumed name again and cheating people out of money." Tears trickled down the woman's cheeks.

Mrs. Melody put an arm around her old school friend. "Please don't feel so bad about this. I'm sure your brother will be found and will make amends. Let's go out to his house and see if we can find something to help solve the mystery."

They set out at once for Rawley Banister's. When they reached the hilltop, the place seemed peaceful. In the bright sun the house did not appear so formidable.

Mrs. Carrier took the key from her handbag and inserted it in the front-door lock. She turned the knob and the heavy door swung inward. The hall was dark but daylight penetrated for a short distance.

"Oh! What's that?" Mrs. Melody cried out, pulling back.

All of them heard a strange whirring sound. The next instant a weird metal figure whizzed across the hall, then went out of sight. But in a couple of moments it returned and shot past the callers.

"It's a robot!" Nancy exclaimed. "He must be guarding the place."

The visitors hesitated to walk in, but presently

the robot disappeared through a swinging door at the rear of the hallway.

"I wonder if he's coming back," Mrs. Carrier said fearfully. "Rawley didn't warn me that eerie things might happen here!"

Nancy was puzzled why the tape recorder at the door had not worked. "Maybe the knocker sets it off." But when she rapped with it, there was no voice. "Strange," she murmured.

Just then the robot came through the swinging door. This time the figure on wheels stopped beside a slanting column on top of which was a coach lamp. With one hand the robot turned on the lamp. The funny little mechanical man then went toward the front door and snapped on the switch for a ceiling fixture.

"Oh!" Mrs. Carrier burst out. "I can't believe it!"

Mr. Drew smiled. "He seems harmless enough."

Mrs. Melody pointed to a broad staircase. It was the most fantastic one any of them had ever seen. It twisted and turned every few feet. Even the spindles were not upright; some slanted forward, others backward.

On the left side the railing ended in a very attractive newel. The other banister stopped about three steps from the floor and ran into a wall. The staircase had not been centered. The whole thing gave the entrance hallway an unbalanced look.

"Why do you suppose your brother planned all this unusual architecture?" Mr. Drew asked Mrs. Carrier.

"I haven't the faintest idea," she answered. "As a little boy Rawley used to build queer-looking things with his blocks, and later with metal construction toys. He made buildings, bridges, and strange cars and planes."

Mr. Drew nodded. "That figures. This place was sort of your brother's dream house."

"I suppose so," Mrs. Carrier agreed. "He wanted to see how much he could build things off balance and without them toppling over."

Nancy continued to stare at the crooked staircase. Smiling, she said, "Sliding down that banister would be a terrific challenge."

"I certainly wouldn't want to attempt it," said Mrs. Melody.

The walls of the entrance hall were papered in a gold-and-black floral pattern. There was only one picture. It hung just above the end of the unfinished banister, and was a framed Oriental hand-embroidered wall decoration. The visitors walked over to it and studied the weird design.

"One, two, three, four, five, six, seven serpents," Nancy counted, "all intertwined. They look greedy and horrible."

"Yes," her father said. "And each one is eating poisonous food. Some are flowers, others snakes. I recognize this plant as deadly nightshade."

"And isn't one of the serpents swallowing a poisonous snake?" Nancy asked. "I think it's a cottonmouth."

Before anyone could answer, the callers were startled by an explosion beyond the swinging door.

"Oh, what happened?" Mrs. Melody exclaimed.

The group stood frozen. If they rushed in to find out, would they perhaps be trapped and never get out of this weird house alive?

CHAPTER III

Telltale Evidence

THE visitors finally decided to find out what had happened behind the swinging door but to do so cautiously. Mr. Drew insisted upon looking first. Carefully he opened the door and peered inside.

"I guess everything's safe," he said and motioned the others to follow him. Beyond was a large kitchen and in the center of the floor lay the robot, its head off!

"My goodness!" Mrs. Melody exclaimed. "Is he—is he—dead?"

Mr. Drew smiled. "At least he has been beheaded," he answered. "But the rest of his body may be 'hot.' "

"What do you mean?" Mrs. Carrier asked.

The lawyer explained that he did not know exactly how the robot worked. It was possible the figure was charged with electricity and should not be touched.

"Let's find out!" Nancy suggested and began pulling out kitchen drawers. Finally she found what she was looking for—a long-handled wooden spoon.

"Perfect," her father said. "This is a nonconductor. We'll soon know if our little friend is hot!" He began poking into the neck of the robot and announced, "Here is a tape."

Further exploration revealed that many wires and pulleys ran to the robot's arms and legs.

"Evidently," Nancy remarked, "this little man was programmed to do certain things, even to warn visitors away."

Mrs. Melody looked puzzled. "But if nobody was here, how did it start?"

"I'm not sure," Mr. Drew replied. "Some robots are set off by heat, even the warmth of a human body. Others are designed to react to sound. I suspect it is sound in this case."

Mrs. Carrier said, "You mean that when we came into the house the pitch of our voices activated the robot?"

"Possibly," Mr. Drew replied.

Nancy took a flashlight from her purse and shone it down inside the figure. "A lot of wires are broken," she said, "so we can be doubly sure this creature won't hurt us. But I do think he should be fixed. I have a hunch he's going to figure big in our mystery."

She opened other drawers and presently came

upon reels of tapes, marked with numbers and letters.

Nancy turned to Mrs. Carrier. "Is there a good electrician in town who would come and repair the robot?" she asked.

Several seconds went by before the woman replied. "I dislike the thought of bringing strangers here," she said. "But if you really feel that the robot might be a clue to the whereabouts of my brother, I'll agree. There's a very good electrician in Mountainville. I'll get in touch with him."

Nancy thanked her and then suggested that they search the house. The kitchen was modern with an outside door which had a Yale lock.

"I hope we don't have any more scares," Mrs. Melody said.

On one side of the center hall, in back of a den, was the dining room with crudely made but symmetrical furniture. Its walls contained several paintings, all of queer-looking undersea creatures, some with long tentacles.

The living room was on the opposite side of the hall. It was furnished with ultramodern pieces and had a large convex bookcase on the hall side.

As the group mounted the zigzag steps to the second floor, Nancy and Mrs. Melody began to giggle. The woman said, "This is like climbing a stony mountain trail that twists and turns every few feet."

The bedrooms and a study proved to be comfortable but filled with weird and ghoulish silver figurines. In the room where Rawley apparently slept, the bed had a high peak under the middle of the spread.

Mrs. Melody remarked, "Sally, do you suppose your brother slept with his legs draped over that barrier?"

"He's tall enough to," Mrs. Carrier answered.

Nancy examined the bed and found that it contained a jointed mattress which could be moved electrically. She pushed one of the control buttons and the mattress descended to a flat position.

"That looks better," Mrs. Carrier said.

While the others gazed at the ultramodern etchings on the walls, Nancy walked over to a fireplace which looked as if it had been used frequently. Ashes and half-burned logs lay just inside the hearth. A slender, rounded, brass box stood at the edge. Nancy opened it and gasped.

Inside were a dozen taper matches that looked like the one she had found on the balcony of the motel!

Not wishing to upset Mrs. Carrier, Nancy went over to her father, took his hand, and unobtrusively guided him to the brass box. Then she walked back to the two women. Mr. Drew lifted the lid and gave Nancy a knowing look as he closed it.

A few minutes later Mrs. Carrier and Mrs. Melody left the room and went downstairs. The Drews discussed the clue of the taper match.

"It certainly seems to indicate that Rawley set the fires and stole the papers," Mr. Drew stated.

"To make sure," said Nancy, "I'll take one of these fireplace matches along and compare it with the match I have at the motel."

When she and her father joined the two women at the foot of the crooked stairway, Mrs. Carrier said she was worried about leaving the property unguarded. "There's a lot of valuable art work and silver pieces in this house. What do you think I should do, Mr. Drew?"

The lawyer suggested a watchman. They found a telephone and directory in the kitchen and looked up the name of an employment agency in Mountainville.

As Mrs. Carrier dialed the number, she gazed at the headless robot and remarked, "That thing gives me the creeps! . . . Hello. Tepper Employment Agency?"

"Yes. Frank Furness speaking."

Mrs. Carrier gave the address of Rawley Banister's house and said she would like to hire a watchman to guard the place day and night.

"I'll call you back," Mr. Furness said, "after I contact some names on our list."

Twenty minutes later the phone rang. "I'm sorry, madam, but I couldn't find anyone to help you out. You know, that place has a reputation of being a crazy house. The men I asked said they wouldn't go there for a million dollars!" He hung up.

When Mrs. Carrier repeated the conversation, Nancy smiled. "Don't worry. If guards are afraid to come here, I'm sure burglars would be too."

"I hope you're right," Mrs. Carrier said with a deep sigh. "I suppose we may as well leave."

The front door was securely locked and the visitors walked to Nancy's car. Mr. Drew slid into the driver's seat. Nancy sat next to him. On the way back to town, he said:

"Mrs. Melody and I must leave directly after lunch."

Nancy was disappointed. She had just become involved in the baffling mystery and now she must give it up. To her surprise Mr. Drew said, "Nancy, if you are willing to stay here, I'd like you to continue work on the case."

The young sleuth's eyes lighted up. "Dad, that's terrific! You know I'll do my best—"

"Not so fast," her father said, patting Nancy on the shoulder. "There's one big condition that goes with this."

"What is it, Dad?"

Mr. Drew said he would like Nancy to call her friends Bess and George to see if they could come and stay with her. "If they can't, you'll have to return home with me."

Bess Marvin and George Fayne were cousins. The two girls had been friends of Nancy's for many years. They often accompanied her when she was working on mysteries and always proved to be of great help.

After dropping Mrs. Carrier at her home, the Drews and Mrs. Melody returned to the motel. Nancy immediately phoned George and asked if she and Bess could spend a few days with her in Mountainville to solve a mystery. Nancy mentioned the motel fire.

"If you girls can come, please call Hannah and have her pack a suitcase of clothes for me." George said she would do this and let Nancy know the plans.

During lunch she received a call from George saying she and Bess could come. They were getting a ride with a relative who would pass through Mountainville about five o'clock.

Nancy told her father the good news. He wished the three girls luck and added with a chuckle, "Mrs. Melody, I always give Nancy hard assignments and always with great confidence that she will come up with the right answers." He smiled affectionately at his daughter.

Nancy smiled back, though she did not feel confident about solving this mystery. She had been given the difficult task of learning the whereabouts of a man who had not only disappeared but had left behind a frightening robot!

She drove her father and Mrs. Melody to a bus stop directly after lunch and then went on a shopping tour to look at fall clothes. If she were going to stay in Mountainville for some time, there might be cool days. For a while Nancy's mind was taken completely off the mystery as she tried on sports suits. She decided to purchase a tan suit, then bought shoes to match.

Later, Nancy stopped at the police station and the firehouse to inquire if there was any new information on Rawley Banister or the person who had set the three blazes at the motel. In each case the answer was no.

Leaving the firehouse, Nancy looked at her wrist watch. She still had plenty of time before Bess and George would arrive, and decided to walk back leisurely to the motel.

As she gazed into an art-shop window, a man's voice behind her said, "Hello, Nancy Drew."

She turned to face a stranger. Nancy was sure she had never seen him before.

"I guess you don't remember me," said the tall,

thin man with a rather pinched face. He was in his thirties, Nancy judged, and the thought also ran through her mind that he could use a good meal!

He laughed and said, "I met you at Emerson College, where I used to teach. I'm Clyde Mead."

Still Nancy could not remember him. Emerson was the school her friend Ned Nickerson attended and she had been to many football games and house parties there. She tried her best to recall this man but failed.

"You're not at the college now?" Nancy asked.

"No."

"What do you do?"

"I'm a professional fundraiser. At present I'm working on an appeal you'll certainly be interested in."

The longer the man talked, the more suspicious Nancy became of his former connection with Emerson College and of his sincerity. She decided to get away from him as quickly as possible.

CHAPTER IV

The Annoying Salesman

DETERMINED to end the conversation, Nancy turned and said to Mr. Mead, "I must go back to the motel now." She looked at her watch. "I'm expecting friends soon."

Nancy's hopes of getting rid of the man vanished. Taking her arm and smiling most ingratiatingly, he said, "Let me take you there. I'm so glad I ran into you again."

Not wishing to make a scene on the street, Nancy allowed Mr. Mead to accompany her, but casually shook off his hand. When they reached the motel, he walked into the lobby with her.

"Oh good!" he said. "They're serving tea. Suppose you and I sit down and have some. I know you'll be interested in what I'm doing. I'll tell you about it. Have you ever been on an Indian reservation?"

"Yes."

"Then you know that many of the Indians make only a bare living from farming, and their children lack many comforts of life."

Though concerned about the plight of the Indians, Nancy was exasperated by the man's aggressive manner. Just as she decided that the only way to get rid of Mr. Mead was to go to her room, he summoned a waitress and ordered two cups of tea and a plate of cookies. The young detective's face reddened in anger, but again she did not want to call attention to herself and reluctantly sat down.

Once more she looked at her watch. If only Bess and George would come and free her from this man! There was still half an hour before they would arrive.

Mr. Mead said, "My sympathy for the children on the reservations was aroused during a recent trip out West. The poor little ones need so many things—clothing, books, games, toys, and even food."

He pulled a pamphlet from his pocket. Distress and poverty were shown in a series of pictures.

"Aren't they pathetic?" he asked. "Miss Drew, surely you can't refuse to help them. I know a fine little fellow who could use some money from you to buy clothes and food."

Nancy was touched by the depressing pictures, but did not reply. As she looked off into space, she was relieved to see Bess and George coming through the front door.

Nancy jumped up, saying, "Excuse me, Mr. Mead. My friends have arrived."

She rushed over to the two girls and hugged them. Bess, blond and pretty, was slightly plump. George, slender and athletic-looking, enjoyed her boyish name. She too was attractive and had short black hair.

"You made good time!" Nancy exclaimed.

"Not much traffic," Bess replied. "My aunt knew a shortcut, and here we are!"

Nancy had not noticed that Clyde Mead had followed her. Bess and George looked at Nancy in surprise.

The man did not wait for an introduction. He put out his hand. "You girls are friends of Nancy Drew?" he asked. "I'm so glad to meet you. The name is Clyde Mead, but just call me Clyde."

Thinking that Nancy had accepted his friendship, the cousins shook hands cordially. Nancy was even more angry with him now. Ignoring Mead, she asked Bess and George to register, then led the way to the room the three girls would share.

When they were inside, Bess asked, "Who's your new flame?"

Nancy told them how the two had met. "Maybe Clyde Mead is working for a good cause, but he's the most annoying man I've ever known! It would please me if I never see him again!"

"Why, Nancy," George said, "I haven't seen you this mad in a long time! Tell us all about him—where he's from and everything."

When Nancy had finished, George said, "I don't blame you for being suspicious. He doesn't seem like the professor type. Let's forget him. We want to hear all about the mystery you're working on."

Nancy told her friends how the Melodys had been swindled, then went on to describe Rawley Banister's mysterious house with the robot guard, the amazingly crooked staircase, and the bizarre serpent picture.

"It's the craziest place I've ever heard of," George remarked. "Just the same, I can hardly wait to see it."

Bess said she was not so sure she wanted to go inside the house. "It sounds spooky and dangerous. That robot may have more tricks up his sleeve!"

Nancy laughed. "Not until he gets his wires fixed and his head back on!"

She added that Mrs. Carrier was going to find an electrician to repair the robot.

"I'd like to be there to see what happens," she said. "How about going out to the house tomorrow morning?"

"Great!" George replied.

Bess said nothing, but was thinking, "I just knew if I came up here, Nancy would be working on something horrendous." Aloud she remarked, "We'd better watch our step in that crazy place. Rawley Banister may have cooked up other things besides the robot."

Nancy spoke of the moat surrounding the house and the story that at times the water in it actually burned.

George laughed. "I don't believe a word of that legend."

The girls dressed for dinner and went downstairs to the pleasant dining room. They were able to get a table in a far corner. Nancy had requested that location to avoid any encounter with Clyde Mead. The three had just ordered when to her dismay she saw him coming toward them.

"Good evening," he said pleasantly and pulled out a chair. "You don't mind if I eat with you? It's such a bore having dinner alone. Don't you agree?"

None of them answered. The waitress took his order, then he began to talk once more about the Indian children he had met.

"Many of them are extremely bright," he said. "Given half a chance to further their education, they might become brilliant scholars, doctors, or engineers."

Within a short time Nancy and George became

bored with Mr. Mead's repetitious conversation, but Bess was fascinated by it. She let her dessert go uneaten.

In desperation Nancy changed the subject. "Mr. Mead, have you ever seen or heard of the unusual house near here owned by Mr. Rawley Banister?"

"No, I haven't. Would you show it to me?"

Nancy was firm in her answer. "I'm sorry but we wouldn't have any time. We'll be busy every single minute during our stay in Mountainville."

When the meal was over, the four walked out of the dining room. Nancy and George led the way. Mr. Mead accompanied Bess, walking a little distance behind the others.

When they reached the lobby, Bess announced that she was going to her room for a minute. "Where shall I meet you girls?"

George replied, "In the gift shop."

She had chosen this place thinking Clyde Mead would not follow her and Nancy. She was right. He walked off in another direction.

Nancy and George went into the shop and wandered around. It was nearly fifteen minutes later when Bess joined them.

"Sorry I took so long," she said.

George grinned. "I thought maybe you'd gone off to some Indian reservation with Mr. Clyde Mead."

Bess made a wry face at her cousin, then asked, "Have you bought anything?"

"Not yet," George replied. "You're the big shopper of this threesome."

"Well, tonight I'm not," Bess replied.

George asked if Bess felt ill.

"Of course not," she said. "To tell the truth, I can't get those poor Indian children out of my mind."

George looked at her cousin sternly. "Forget that man and his Indians! How do we know he's on the level?"

Bess did not reply. She waited patiently while Nancy and George bought neckties as gifts for their fathers. Then the three went to their room.

At once Nancy said, "Want to see a real clue I picked up here last night in connection with the mystery?"

"Sure do," George replied. Bess said nothing.

Nancy opened a dresser drawer and took out two taper matches. Holding one in each hand, she measured them, turned and twisted each, and finally said, "They're identical!"

George commented, "Okay, they're identical. Just what does that mean?"

"I found one near the fire. The other is from Rawley Banister's house," Nancy replied. "It's possible he brought some matches from his home and used them to set the fires in the rooms Dad and Mrs. Melody and I had, but lost one in a crack on the balcony." Bess and George gasped in astonishment.

Just then the telephone rang. Nancy picked it up.

A man at the other end asked, "Miss Drew?"

"Yes."

The deep voice continued, "This is Mr. Banister!"

CHAPTER V

The Attack

WHEN the speaker said he was Mr. Banister, Nancy caught her breath. Was this the man she and many others were trying to locate?

Her heart pounded as she said, "Yes, Mr. Banister."

The caller went on, "I'm Thomas Banister, a brother to Rawley."

With a sigh Nancy relaxed. Bess and George, having seen their friend's sudden change of expression, wondered who was telephoning.

Mr. Banister said, "I understand your father is trying to locate my brother. That's true, isn't it?"

"I believe so," Nancy replied guardedly.

"Well, listen," the caller went on, "you give this message to your father. I didn't know where to phone him. That's why I called you. Tell him that he's to stop work on the search at once!"

"Stop work—?"

"That's what I said. This whole thing is a family matter and will be taken care of by us. We don't need any other help. Is that clear?"

"Quite."

Mr. Banister stated that he did not want to discuss the case further. "Drop it! Tell your father we're sorry to have caused any inconvenience." The caller hung up.

Nancy sat staring at the ceiling. She thought, "The end of a beautiful mystery for me!"

She turned to Bess and George and relayed the conversation. George knew how disappointed Nancy was and refrained from making any comment.

Bess said with relief, "It's probably better this way. I'm sure, Nancy, that you would have ended up with some horrible thing happening to you."

Without replying, Nancy dialed the Drew home. Her father was there and she told him about Thomas Banister's message.

"I'm amazed," Mr. Drew said. "Mrs. Carrier seemed so eager to have us work on the mystery."

"What shall we do?" Nancy asked.

After a moment's pause her father said, "It was Mr. and Mrs. Melody who engaged me to take on this case. Suppose you phone Mr. Banister and remind him of this. See what he says and then we'll decide upon our next move. Call me back."

Nancy looked up Thomas Banister's number in the directory. As she was about to dial it, the thought suddenly occurred to her that perhaps Thomas Banister had not telephoned. Someone else might have used his name!

She put in the call. A man's voice said, "Hello?"

Nancy asked, "Is this Mr. Thomas Banister?"

"Yes."

"This is Nancy Drew. I'm at the motel. Did you phone me a little while ago?"

"Why no," he replied. "My sister has told me about you. I hope we'll meet soon!"

Nancy told him that someone using his name had telephoned and said her father was to give up the case at once. "He sounded exactly like you," she finished.

The young sleuth could hear a deep sigh at the other end of the line. "It must have been my brother Rawley. Did he say where he was calling from?"

"No, he didn't, Mr. Banister. Then, since you didn't phone," Nancy went on, "you and Mrs. Carrier do want Dad and me to keep on trying to find your brother?"

"Indeed we do. Rawley must make amends. Personally I know nothing about his private affairs. It's my guess, from what my sister tells me, he may have money or valuables stowed away which would take care of all his debts."

Nancy asked Thomas if he had any idea how

Rawley had found out the Drews were on the case.

"No, I haven't," he replied.

After saying good-by, Nancy told Bess and George what Thomas Banister had said, then phoned her father. He too suspected that the call had been made by Rawley. Mr. Drew said he would try to have the call traced, but doubted that this would be possible.

Next Nancy telephoned Mrs. Carrier to see if she and the electrician were going out to Rawley's house the following morning.

"Yes," the woman replied. "And I'm eager to meet Bess and George. Will you pick me up at ten o'clock?" she asked. "Mr. Glassboro, the electrician, will follow in his truck."

When the group reached Rawley's house the next morning, they led Mr. Glassboro to the kitchen and showed him the broken robot.

"Well, that's something!" he exclaimed. "This is a queer house all right and old Robby here just fits in."

"Do you think you can fix him?" Mrs. Carrier asked.

Mr. Glassboro stood the five-foot-tall robot up on its wheeled feet and flashed a light inside. "Humph! There are a lot of broken wires and this tape in here snapped. That's what caused the explosion. When he fell over, his head rolled off."

Nancy showed him the drawer where there were many other tapes.

"Mrs. Carrier, I think I can mend this old fellow—at least, I'll do my best. And splice the broken tape, too."

The others decided to leave the electrician alone and went to the front hall. Mrs. Carrier suggested she and the girls go through Rawley's personal belongings on the second floor.

Nancy agreed it was a good idea. "Maybe we'll find a useful clue," she added.

They climbed the crooked staircase and started their search. The closets contained the usual assortment of clothing, shoes, and sports equipment. There was nothing to indicate that Rawley had strange taste in wearing apparel.

"Apparently he didn't take much with him," Bess remarked. "Not an empty hanger in the place."

In the meantime Mrs. Carrier looked in the pockets of Rawley's clothing. She did not find anything in them and began to rummage through the dresser drawers.

"These are filled with so much stuff it will take forever to go through them," she announced. "It would save time if you girls check the two chests in Rawley's study."

Bess and George offered to do this while Nancy went downstairs to see how the electrician was progressing. As she neared the kitchen,

Nancy thought it strange she did not hear a sound.

"Probably Mr. Glassboro is doing some delicate manipulating with the wires," she murmured.

Nancy swung open the door to the kitchen and then stepped back, shocked. The electrician lay on the floor unconscious! Not far from him stood the robot, its head back on.

"Oh, Mr. Glassboro!" Nancy cried out.

She ran to assist him. As she was about to bend down, a whirring sound started inside the mechanical man and she turned to face him. The next moment the figure raised his two arms and clasped them tightly about Nancy. He began to squeeze her hard.

"Help!" Nancy screamed. "Help!" Then she blacked out.

Upstairs Bess and George heard the cry. "Nancy's in trouble!" Bess exclaimed.

The two girls scurried down the crooked stairway and into the kitchen. Their friend was draped over one arm of the robot.

"We must get her loose!" George said urgently. "Bess, pull one of his arms. I'll yank the other." But neither limb would budge.

"What'll we do?" Bess wailed.

"There's only one thing to do," George replied. "Apparently the tape that set off the robot is still running. We must stop it!"

"Help!" Nancy screamed. "Help!"

She looked around the kitchen at the scattered tools the electrician had been using. Seeing nothing heavy enough, she opened his workbag. Inside was a large wrench. George pulled it out and whacked the robot on the neck again and again.

Finally the whirring stopped. The arms of the mechanical man fell to his sides and he dropped to the floor. Nancy sagged into Bess's arms. Gently her friends placed her on the floor.

"The robot must have done the same thing to Mr. Glassboro," George said. "Quick! Get some ice!"

Bess dashed across the room to the refrigerator and soon was putting cold cloths on Nancy's head and chafing her wrists. George was doing the same to the electrician. In a few minutes both revived. They blinked their eyes and looked gratefully at Bess and George.

"What happened?" George asked.

Mr. Glassboro said that he had repaired the robot and wanted to find out if he worked. The electrician had taken a tape at random from the drawer and inserted it. "Robby had hardly started whirring when one of his arms moved up and gave me the neatest uppercut I've ever seen. It knocked me out."

George smiled. "In other words you were kayoed by a mechanical man!" The others laughed.

As Nancy told what had happened to her, the electrician and the girls gazed at the fallen robot.

Mr. Glassboro remarked, "If we try out any more of these tapes, we'd better put old Robby in a cage! But I'll repair the one that caused the explosion, so it will be safe to use."

The mechanical man was dragged to his feet. Mr. Glassboro removed the head and looked inside the body. He said the wires seemed to be all right, but the tape had been ruined by George's vigorous whacking.

"Thank goodness!" said Bess. "This thing is really dangerous!"

It was evident to the girls that Rawley Banister kept the robot on hand for protection. Was he so deeply involved in swindles that he feared for his life? they wondered.

Mr. Glassboro spoke up. "This is no play toy. I'll explain how he works, then I think he should be hidden. How about this closet here?"

There was a key in the door, which George unlocked. The electrician briefed the girls on how to use the tapes, then rolled Robby into the closet and locked it.

By this time Mrs. Carrier had come downstairs. She had not heard the commotion and was thunderstruck to learn what had happened.

"You girls must be careful," she said. "And Mr. Glassboro, I certainly am sorry that you had such a misadventure."

The man smiled as he started to mend the tape. "It's all in a day's work," he said, "but I must admit I'm not used to being knocked out by a mechanical man."

He finished quickly and left in his truck. The others decided to go also and started across the bridge.

In the excitement Nancy had forgotten to bring her handbag from the second floor. Mrs. Carrier unlocked the front door and the young sleuth hurried inside. By now she had learned how to go up the crooked stairway quickly, and was back in a few minutes.

Mrs. Carrier and the girls crossed the narrow bridge. As the group headed for Nancy's car, they saw a man walking up the woods road.

Mrs. Carrier caught her breath. "It's Rawley!" she exclaimed.

CHAPTER VI

Hidden Workshop

To the amazement of the foursome, the man coming up the woods road did not turn and run off when he spotted them. Instead, Rawley Banister strode forward at a brisk pace.

Nancy, Bess, and George looked at one another in amazement. By now he had surely seen the group, yet he made no move to flee.

"I can't believe it!" George whispered. "He's walking right into the lion's cage!"

Suddenly Mrs. Carrier burst into laughter. The girls stared at her questioningly.

"That's not Rawley! He's Thomas!"

"You mean—you mean—" Bess began.

Mrs. Carrier said that her two brothers looked very much alike. At a distance it was hard to distinguish between them.

"I wasn't expecting Thomas to come here. He didn't say anything about it and once told me he would never set foot in the house!"

Nancy smiled. "Everyone is allowed to change his mind, don't you think? Besides, your brother may have some important news."

"Hello," Thomas Banister said cordially. He was a handsome, dark-haired man in his middle thirties.

After Mrs. Carrier introduced the three girls, he said, "Miss Drew and I became acquainted over the telephone. You're all probably wondering why I came here—especially on foot."

His sister said, "It must be for some special reason. Would you like to go inside the house and talk it over?"

"If you're not in a hurry," Thomas replied, "I think it would be a good idea."

"You have a big surprise coming if you've never been here before," George told him as they crossed the bridge and walked to the front entrance.

"So I understand."

Mrs. Carrier opened the door and they all went in. When the ceiling light in the hall was turned on, Thomas's eyes popped in astonishment.

"This is even more fantastic than I imagined," he commented, gazing at the stairway. He shook his head. "I knew my brother was eccentric, but not to this extent."

Bess said, "Wait until you see the robot running around knocking people out!"

Nancy told what had happened to her and to the electrician.

"It seems incredible," Thomas remarked, "but I'm not too surprised to hear it. From the time Rawley was a little boy he was always building weird and ingenious things.

"His talent and education as an engineer should have been turned to good use," he went on. "It's most unfortunate that he chose to lead the wrong kind of life. Our family argued with him and tried to persuade him to do something worth while, but he'd always laugh off the suggestions."

Nancy led the way into the kitchen and unlocked the closet door. Stripped of his animation, the robot seemed forlorn and beaten.

"From what you've told me," Thomas said, "I think this is a good place to keep him out of mischief."

The group went into the living room and sat down. Thomas proceeded to tell the others why he had come to Rawley's house.

"When I learned that you people weren't at the motel or at my sister's, I assumed you were here, so I drove out. At the foot of the hill my car ran out of gas. And here's some disturbing news."

Thomas said he had been visited by Mr. and Mrs. Stuart Aldrin from New York City. Like Mrs. Melody they had been cheated by Rawley, who had been using an assumed name. They had been unable to track him down.

"But they saw the newspaper picture of him," Thomas went on, "and came directly to me. They're demanding the return of a large sum of money plus damages."

Mrs. Carrier frowned. "For what?" she asked.

Thomas said that apparently Rawley had helped himself to certain identification cards and business papers from a realty company in New York City. "They handle the rentals of luxury apartment houses."

According to the Aldrins' story, Rawley had posed as a member of the firm and had taken the Aldrins to a large building. He had informed the doorman that Mr. and Mrs. Cooper, who were out of town at the moment, were giving up their apartment and the Aldrins were interested.

"Rawley showed the Cooper apartment to which he had a key. Evidently he had taken it from the realty-company office."

"Where does the large sum of money come in?" Mrs. Carrier asked.

"The Aldrins said they would take the apartment and then were told that they would have to pay three months' rent in advance. Mr. Aldrin agreed and Rawley made out a receipt on the realty company's billhead and gave them a fake lease."

Thomas said Rawley had told his clients there

was a bonus payment in connection with taking over the apartment before the Coopers' lease ran out. Mr. Aldrin had also paid that fee.

George spoke up. "It seems to me Mr. Aldrin wasn't on the ball. He should have investigated Rawley's story to see if it were true before he turned over the money."

Thomas smiled. "I'm afraid there are too many people in this world who are easily taken."

"I suppose so," George agreed.

Thomas went on, "The most shocking part of the story is that the Aldrins insist my sister and I make good on every penny they gave to Rawley!"

"We can't do that!" Mrs. Carrier cried out. "We've already paid out a lot of money because of him. Besides, there's no telling how many more people may make demands on us."

"I'm afraid you're right," Thomas said. "Legally, of course, none of these people can collect from us. I keep hoping that money or other valuables of Rawley's will be found to reimburse these claimants."

"You mean hidden in this house?" Bess asked.

"Probably."

Mrs. Carrier asked if her brother would like to look over the rest of the place.

"Yes, indeed."

They walked into the hall. Thomas stood still and gazed at the crooked stairway. The next second he bounded up the steps, twisting and turning as he went. He had almost reached the top when he tripped. The next moment he lost his balance and came rolling down!

"Oh!" Mrs. Carrier cried out.

Nancy made a leap for the stairway and dashed up. She was able to stop Thomas before he crashed to the bottom. He got up sheepishly and sat down on one of the steps.

"Are you all right?" Nancy asked him.

"I guess so," he replied. "Hereafter I'll have more respect for this crazy invention of my brother's."

Mrs. Carrier and the other two girls came up the steps to make sure Thomas was all right. He insisted that he was.

"I probably have a few bruises, but that's all. No broken bones."

The group went upstairs. While Thomas made a tour of the rooms, Nancy again looked for a clue to the missing man's whereabouts.

She mentioned her search to Thomas, who said, "I have a suggestion. Maybe there's a computer hidden some place. Rawley would be capable of making his own program tapes for the robot. If we find the computer, possibly we will discover something that would help us track down Rawley."

A hunt was started. Nancy told Thomas that none of the searchers had investigated the basement. They found a concealed door at the back of the pantry which opened onto a stairway leading downward. There were many wall switches which lighted the place brilliantly.

"I'm sure Rawley worked down here," Thomas remarked.

There were several rooms. One had a sliding door which contained a large computer and a small one.

"You were right about your brother doing the programming himself," Nancy told Thomas. The group searched but found no clue to the man's whereabouts.

The other rooms were inspected but yielded nothing of value except a small printing press.

As the group returned to the first floor, Nancy kept telling herself that there must be other secrets in this house. Where were they and how was she going to find them?

"Rawley Banister is clever, if not honest," she thought. "He probably figured it would be a great joke on his family to make them hunt for any valuables that might be hidden here."

She stopped to gaze once more at the crooked stairway. Why had it been built this way? Why did the one railing end part way up in a wall? Why was the hall not balanced?

"We'd better go," Mrs. Carrier called. "I don't know about the rest of you, but I'm starved."

Bess laughed. "Me too."

Thomas invited them to lunch.

"But I need a lift to the foot of the hill." He chuckled ruefully. "When I ran out of gas, I signaled a passing motorist to send somebody there and put in a few gallons and charge it to me. I hope he did."

Thomas climbed into Nancy's car and they all rode to where he had left his. Fortunately, gasoline had been put in and he led the way to an attractive restaurant near a river on the outskirts of Mountainville.

As they walked in, Thomas said, "That couple just coming from the dining room are Mr. and Mrs. Aldrin. I don't want to talk to them now."

He could not escape them, however. Spotting him at the entrance to the room, the couple hurried to his side.

"So we meet again!" said Mr. Aldrin. "Is this lady your sister?"

Thomas nodded, then introduced the group to the Aldrins.

"Have you come to any conclusions about reimbursing my wife and me?" the man asked in a loud voice.

"No," Thomas replied. "If I have any news, I'll get in touch with you."

There was an embarrassing pause. Suddenly Bess broke the silence. "Nancy Drew is a detective. Maybe you'd like her to work on your case."

Mr. Aldrin's answer was a loud haw-haw, followed by, "She's only a girl!"

His wife laughed uproariously. "Can you imagine such a thing? I can see a headline now—TEEN-AGE GIRL CAPTURES CON MAN!"

Nancy was embarrassed. Her face flushed with anger as patrons in the restaurant stared.

CHAPTER VII

Burning Water

"COME!" said Thomas Banister.

He took Nancy by the arm and led her to a secluded table in a corner of the restaurant. His sister and the other girls followed.

When they were seated, Mrs. Carrier burst out, "Those people are dreadful! How rude of them to make such a remark!"

"I agree," said Bess. "I'd just like to tell them what a terrific detective Nancy is!"

George recommended that they forget all about the Aldrins. "We don't even know if they're honest," she remarked. "They could have made up the whole story about being cheated by your brother in order to get money from you."

Thomas nodded as a waitress approached them. After menus had been passed around, he asked, "What would you all like to eat?"

Mrs. Carrier chose cream of tomato soup and chicken salad.

Bess asked haltingly, "Would you mind if I concentrate on dessert?" She hesitated a moment, then said, "Just a small hamburger and a large fudge nut sundae with a piece of cake?"

Nancy expected a tart comment from George about her plumpish cousin's selections, but she said nothing. Apparently George only criticized Bess when the three girls were alone.

Thomas smiled and said if that was what Bess wanted, she certainly should have it. The others ordered simple luncheons and the waitress went off.

A few minutes later Bess murmured, "Guess what! Mrs. Aldrin is coming our way."

"What!" Mrs. Carrier exclaimed.

The woman who had been so sarcastic and unpleasant a short time before smiled affably as she approached the table.

"I came to apologize," she said, looking at Nancy. "It was rude of my husband and me to make fun of your ability as a detective. We realized afterward that we had heard of your father and you. Please forgive us and try to find the man who swindled us."

"I think," Nancy answered, "that you should consult my father. He's a lawyer. As you said, I'm only a teen-age detective."

"But," Mrs. Aldrin said, "I understand you are

very clever. Exactly how much do you charge an hour?"

Nancy's eyes flashed. "If you have heard about me, you must know that I'm strictly an amateur. I work on mysteries because I enjoy them and do not accept money for solving them. I still say you should consult my father. Yours is a legal matter."

Mrs. Aldrin seemed lost for an answer. She looked toward the doorway where her husband was standing and beckoned him to come over. He walked to the table, an expansive smile on his face.

His wife said, "Nancy Drew tells me that our case should be handled by her father."

"Oh yes?" Mr. Aldrin said. "Well, my wife and I have decided to give it to both of you. Shall I get in touch with your father or will you, Miss Drew?"

Nancy said she would prefer having Mr. Aldrin make the contact. "If Dad wants me to work on the case, he can let me know."

Mr. Aldrin did not comment. Instead he said, "I have been doing a little detective work myself. I went back to the apartment house where the Coopers live and talked with the doorman. He said he had seen the impostor at a sports event. He had immediately told a policeman about him, but the faker had disappeared by that time."

Although Nancy felt that this was a very slim

clue, she remarked, "Perhaps the doorman will see the suspect again and have him arrested."

Thomas spoke up. "If we hear anything about Rawley's whereabouts, we'll get in touch with you. I have your card so I know where to find you."

The Aldrins went off when the waitress appeared with a tray of food. While eating, Nancy and her friends tried not to talk about the mystery but it kept popping up.

Finally Nancy said, "Do you think that perhaps Rawley comes back to his house at night when he is sure no one will be around?"

"It's possible," Thomas replied. "Tell you what. Suppose we go out there tonight. I'll pick you up at eight o'clock."

"Great!" Nancy said "We'll be ready."

When the girls reached their motel room, Nancy received a telephone call from Thomas Banister. He said a business matter had come up and he would be unable to take the group to his brother's house that evening.

"Perhaps we can make it tomorrow night," he suggested. "I'll call you." A few minutes later the phone rang again. Nancy answered.

"Ned!" she cried out in delight.

"Hi! How is everything?" he asked. Nancy was fond of the tall, handsome football player from Emerson College and dated him almost exclusively.

"How did you find out I was here?"

"From Mrs. Gruen," Ned replied.

"I left home in such a hurry I didn't have time to let you know," Nancy said. "And since I've been here, it seems as if every minute has been taken up with the new mystery."

She was surprised and pleased when Ned announced that he and Burt and Dave, George's and Bess's favorite dates, were free that evening and would like to drive over.

"Wonderful!" Nancy said. "Will you stay overnight?"

Ned thought this would be best since it was a rather long distance from where the boys were working. Fortunately they had the following day off from their summer jobs of selling insurance.

"The company is giving its employees a holiday. We'd rather spend it with you girls than go on the company's picnic."

Nancy chuckled. "And I'll bet you're hoping to help on the mystery."

Ned admitted this was true. "I'll hang up now," he added. "See you later."

When Nancy told Bess and George the good news, they were thrilled.

George said, "How about the six of us going out to Rawley's house tonight? I'd like to show the boys that fantastic place."

Bess added, "And if the con man is there, I'd

rather the boys capture him than we girls."

The three arrived at the motel just before eight o'clock. Burt Eddleton was a short blond husky youth. He liked George because of her interest in sports. Dave Evans was also blond but rangy. He had smiling green eyes and liked to tease Bess. Over ice cream sundaes Nancy briefed the boys on the mystery.

"Wow!" Ned exclaimed. "This case sounds like a weirdo."

"Wait until you see the funny house and the crazy stairway that the Crooked Banister built," Bess said.

The boys looked at her, puzzled. She giggled and explained. "Rawley Banister, it seems, was always getting into trouble. He nicknamed himself the Crooked Banister."

George added, "And the stairway in his house is as crooked as he is."

"Let's go!" Ned urged.

The young people got into his car and set off. Nancy said they would have to pick up the key from Mrs. Carrier, and directed Ned to her house. Nancy hurried inside and explained.

"Of course you have my permission to go there," Mrs. Carrier said. "And I'm glad the boys are going along. I'll get the key."

Nancy slipped it into her handbag and returned to the car. Twenty minutes later they were driving up the wooded road that led to

Rawley's house. By the time they pulled into the clearing at the top of the hill, the moon was shining brightly and the fantastic house stood out clearly. But what interested them most was the reddish glow in the deep moat.

"The water's on fire!" Nancy exclaimed as everyone jumped from the car.

Bess, who was closer to the moat, suddenly cried out, "The bridge is gone!"

"But what could have happened to it?" George burst out. "Did it fall into the water and burn up?"

"I doubt that," Nancy said. "It was a metal bridge, remember? It couldn't catch on fire."

Bess spoke up. "Do you think it was dragged away?"

Nancy studied the ground for evidence of this. There were no marks.

George asked practically, "How are we going to get across to the house?"

"That's a good question," Dave answered.

"I have an idea," Nancy spoke up. "These woods are full of saplings. If we could find some that are tall enough to reach across the moat, we could build our own bridge."

Bess asked, "But how could you cut them down? Unless Ned has an axe in his car."

"I don't," he replied. "But most saplings bend easily and if you push them far enough they will crack off. Come on, fellows. Let's see what we can do."

The six young people went into the woods. In the bright moonlight they had no trouble finding tall, slender young trees and soon had felled several. They lugged them to the edge of the moat and one by one dropped the upper section of each onto the far side. Soon a reasonably stable bridge was constructed.

"I'll go over first to be sure it's safe," Ned offered.

"Oh, Ned," Bess called, "don't take a chance! You might fall into the fire! Wait until the flames die down."

Ned paused a moment. "Suppose all of you hold the saplings in place so they can't roll. I'm sure I'll be all right."

He inched along the crude bridge to the other side, then turned and shouted, "Okay, everybody!"

One by one the young people crossed to the lawn in front of the house. Nancy thought of Hannah Gruen's remark about her getting into hot water. She had come close to doing so!

Burt said, "Do you think it was Rawley who got rid of the bridge? And if so, is he here or did he run away?"

Nancy spoke up. "Since Rawley sent a key to his sister and said she's in charge, I doubt that he'd destroy her only means of getting across to the house."

"Then who did it?" Dave asked. "Somebody caused the fire on that water."

All were convinced that if Rawley were in the house, he would do one of two things: hide from them or try to harm them, perhaps using the robot.

"I don't think we should go in," Bess stated flatly. "Let's surround the house and wait for Rawley to come out."

"But suppose he isn't here?" Nancy countered. "You know, all this might have been done by someone else—either a pal or an enemy of his."

After debating what to do, Ned suggested that they take a vote as to whether they would enter the house or not. There were five votes for going inside and only one for staying outdoors. That was Bess's.

Nancy inserted the key into the front-door lock and Ned pushed it open. Without stepping inside, Nancy reached around to turn on the switch of the hall light. No one was in sight, and the robot did not appear.

Hearing a slight sound in back of the group, Burt looked over his shoulder. The next instant he yelled, "Look! A man is running away from here!"

The others turned in time to see a tall figure in a raincoat and hat pulled low. He reached the moat and started across the sapling bridge.

"That must be Rawley!" George cried out.

A fearful thought came to Bess. "He may ruin our bridge and we'll never get away from here!"

All the young people rushed toward the saplings, ready to hold them down, should the man try to remove them. The fellow looked back once, but did not pause. He reached the other side of the moat and plunged into the woods.

"After him!" Ned ordered. "You girls stay here. Come on, boys! We must catch that man!"

CHAPTER VIII

Vanished!

THE three girls kept an alert watch, ready to ward off any attack by a lurking enemy.

Meanwhile, Ned, Burt, and Dave crashed through the woods. They could hear the fugitive not far ahead, but despite the brilliant moonlight, they could not see him.

Suddenly the man stopped. Was he hiding, or lying in wait for the boys?

"One thing is sure," Ned remarked. "That fellow knows this area better than we do." The boys stood still and listened intently. Now there was not a sound.

"I guess we'll have to give up," Burt replied. A second later he exclaimed, "Listen!"

Not far below they could hear a motor start up.

"There's your answer," Dave said. "That guy

had a car parked down there and we lost him."

Disappointed, the three climbed the hill and reported to the girls.

"Never mind," said Bess. "No telling what he might have done to you. Even in the moonlight this place seems creepy. I kept imagining eyes looking at me from the windows in the zigzag house."

Dave laughed. "Let's go in and see who belongs to the eyes."

Ned looked into the moat. "The fire's out. Probably oil was poured on the water and set ablaze. It didn't last long."

Nancy suggested that two of the group should guard the sapling bridge, while the others went inside to investigate the premises. George and Burt agreed to remain outside.

The four other young people stepped into the entrance hall. Ned remarked that he was sure the staircase had been built in this strange design for some special reason.

"By the way, how old is the house?"

Nancy said Mrs. Carrier had told her it had been put up about ten years ago.

"Before that time, Rawley resided in the old family homestead with his parents. When they passed away, Mrs. Carrier, a widow, went to live there. It was then that Rawley decided to build his own place. I understand he's a bachelor."

"Let's examine the staircase very carefully," Ned suggested.

He and the others tested every step. Dave declared that each one sounded different from the rest. "Listen!"

He went to the top and stomped on each stair as he descended.

Nancy's eyes grew wide. "Why, they're the tones of the scale!" she exclaimed.

Dave grinned. He tried tapping on various treads at intervals.

Bess laughed. "You're playing 'Three Blind Mice.' "

"Right," Dave answered. "Now I'll do 'Mary Had a Little Lamb.' "

Ned began to click each spindle to see if they too produced various sounds. But they showed no variation. Next the two railings were tapped all the way to the bottom but did not indicate any difference in sound.

"Do you suppose," Bess asked, "that maybe we'll come across a sheet of music with a special tune which will reveal the secret of the staircase?"

Everyone thought it was a good possibility and decided to start a search. Nancy and Ned went into the living room. They looked inside books and table drawers and under various pieces of statuary.

Finally Ned remarked, "Those musical steps are probably just another freakish idea of Rawley's."

The couple walked into the hall. Nancy pointed to the Oriental hand-embroidered picture.

"It occurred to me," she remarked, "that this wall hanging might contain the answer to the mystery."

Ned gazed at the embroidered piece in fascination.

"It's pretty sadistic," he said. "A lot of ugly, coiled-up serpents all eating something poisonous!"

"I don't know much about poisons," Nancy admitted. "Are you familiar with them?"

Ned said that in one of his courses he had learned about many of them.

"This plant," he said, pointing, "is the poisonous hemlock. And this one the serpent is chewing is Jimson weed—fatal to cattle who eat it."

Nancy said, "One thing that puzzles me is this object at the bottom of the picture. It looks like an arrow."

"It is an arrow," Ned agreed. "In South America, some tribes make a concoction of poisonous juices into a paste and put it on the tip of an arrow. It's called curare. When the arrow is shot into the body of a person or an animal, the poison is quickly absorbed and causes death in a short time."

"What's this beautiful snake called—the one the fiery serpent is devouring?" Nancy asked.

"Krait," Ned replied. "It's found in Southeast Asia and is extremely poisonous."

Nancy pointed to a small snake. "That's a water moccasin, isn't it?" she asked. "I've seen them in Florida."

Ned nodded. "And this thing you see dangling from the next serpent's mouth I guess you recognize as a black widow spider."

"What we have to do now," said Nancy, "is figure out the meaning of all this. Do you suppose—?"

Her question was cut short by loud yells of distress from Bess and Dave in the kitchen. Nancy and Ned rushed through the swinging door. To their amazement the couple was not there! Standing in the middle of the floor was the robot, its usual vacant stare giving no clue to what had happened.

"How did you get out?" Nancy asked the mechanical man.

She rushed to the closet in which he had been locked. Though the key was still in the door, the door itself was not locked. Nancy yanked it open. There was nothing inside but the assortment of kitchen necessities which had been there earlier.

"Where could Bess and Dave have gone?"

Both she and Ned called their friends' names. There was no answer. They searched the other first-floor rooms but saw no sign of the couple.

Ned frowned. "They couldn't be playing a joke on us, could they?"

Nancy said she doubted this. "I wonder if they took the robot out of that closet and if he could have had anything to do with their disappearance."

"How could he?" Ned asked.

Nancy said she did not know but was going to investigate. "The first thing we should do is put the robot back in the closet, lock it, and for safety hide the key."

Ned pushed the mechanical man inside. After locking the door, Nancy hid the key under a statuette in the living room.

"Unless there's a seeing eye around here," she remarked, "no one will find that key easily."

"Do you think," Ned asked, "the man who ran away from here might have taken the robot out?"

Nancy nodded. "Furthermore, I believe he inserted a tape. When Bess and Dave came into the kitchen, the sound of their voices activated the robot. But what could he have done to them?"

Nancy and Ned stood still, surveying the entire room.

"I don't see a thing," Ned said finally. "Let's

go outdoors. Maybe Bess and Dave ran into the yard."

He and Nancy hurried to the front door and called to George and Burt. "Have you seen Bess and Dave?" Nancy queried.

The answers were no. "Did they come outside?" Burt asked.

"I don't know," Nancy replied. "They've disappeared."

"What!" George exclaimed in alarm.

Burt said he would circle the house and see if he could find the missing couple. In a few minutes he returned, shaking his head.

"Then they must be inside," Ned declared. "Come on, Nancy. We've got to find them."

George and Burt wanted to help, but the bridge had to be guarded. The whole group did not want to be marooned on this side of the moat!

Nancy was convinced that whatever had happened to their missing friends had taken place in the kitchen. She and Ned went directly there. Presently Nancy snapped her fingers.

"See something?" Ned asked.

"Yes," Nancy replied.

She pointed to the floor. It was covered with linoleum in a pattern of large black and white squares. Nancy got down on hands and knees, took her flashlight from a pocket, and beamed it on the various blocks.

Carefully she went over the surface. Ned used his light too. Near the center of the floor Nancy spotted a section where the tiles definitely were not cemented together. She tried to pull one up. It stuck tightly to the floor.

"Ned," she said, running the beam of her flashlight around an area about four feet square, "I believe there's a trap door underneath here! Bess and Dave went through it!"

CHAPTER IX

A Puzzling Discovery

"A TRAP door!" Ned repeated. "But we've been walking all over this place and it didn't open."

"Right," Nancy agreed. "And there isn't any sign of a way to move it."

"Do you think that Bess and Dave fell through, then the door snapped shut?" Ned asked.

"Yes," Nancy replied.

"Perhaps there's a spring hidden somewhere in this kitchen," Ned suggested. "Suppose we see if it's in the cupboards?"

Nancy was thinking hard and did not answer. Finally she said, "I believe Old Robby is programmed to open and close the trap door when it is stepped on. But maybe so long as anybody is down below, he can't pull the trick again."

"And the trap door can't be pushed up from the underside?" Ned asked.

"Evidently not. Unless," Nancy added fearfully, "Bess and Dave fell into such a deep hole, or onto rocks—"

Ned guessed her thought, and his face became very sober. "You think they could be lying down there injured?"

Nancy nodded. "I'm worried, Ned, terribly worried. This was probably all part of Rawley's plan."

"Well, one thing is sure," he answered. "We must get the trap door open. And how are we going to do that if the robot won't work?"

Nancy said they might have to break a section of the floor. "But first I want to try something."

"What?" Ned queried.

Nancy said, "Perhaps the tape came to the end. If we turn it back and start over again, the program may repeat itself."

"It's worth a try," Ned remarked. "But from what you've told me about this sneaky mechanical man, I think we'd better be on the watch for an attack."

Nancy went for the key and unlocked the closet. Ned rolled the robot out and stood him in the exact location where he and Nancy had found him.

They took off his head. The tape had already rewound itself and turned off the main switch. Nancy reset it and instantly the whirring sound began. She and Ned were careful to stay away from the trap-door area. But they wondered if, without their weight on it, that section of the floor would open.

As they stood watching, the two heard a faint click, then a sound as if machinery were working down below. But the door did not move.

"It's just waiting for someone to step on it!" Nancy stated.

She and Ned reached down and pushed with all their might, but carefully avoided stepping on the suspected section. Their efforts were finally rewarded. A trap door opened downward.

"You were right, Nancy," said Ned. He dropped to his knees and called into the dark area below, "Bess! Dave!" There was no answer.

Fearing that the trap door might close again, Nancy disconnected the tape. The whirring sound stopped immediately.

Nancy got down on her knees and shone her flashlight into the depths below. The hole was about six feet deep and had an earthen floor.

She and Ned gave sighs of relief. It was unlikely that Bess and Dave could have been injured by falling through the trap door!

"So far so good," Nancy murmured. "But where did they go?"

The beam of her flashlight revealed an opening to what looked like a tunnel.

"I'll go down," said Ned. "You'd better stay here until I see what's there."

"Oh, I hope you find Bess and Dave and they'll be all right!" she replied anxiously.

The front-door knocker pounded loudly. Nancy said she would answer. George stood there.

"What's going on?" she asked worriedly. "Did you find Bess and Dave?"

"No," Nancy replied, "but we just uncovered a possible clue to where they went. I'll show it to you."

She led the way into the kitchen and George stared in amazement at the open trap door. Nancy explained that the robot had unfastened it.

"George, I'd like to go down and search with Ned. Will you stay here and guard this tricky door? I'm sure it can't close by itself because I've disconnected the tape. But just the same I'd hate to be trapped underground."

"I'll do anything to help find Bess and Dave," George replied. "I'd like to go down there myself, but I'll do as you say and wait up here."

Nancy gripped the edge of the opening and then dropped lightly to the ground below.

"Ned!" she called loudly. Her voice echoed in the tunnel. But presently she received a mumbled reply from him.

"Here I am!"

Nancy hurried along the vaulted corridor,

which was made of stone and earth. There were no openings on either side. The corridor turned sharply to the left.

Just ahead she saw Ned. He was tugging at a heavy door. Nancy hastened toward him.

"You found something?" she called out.

"I think so," he replied hopefully. "This door must lead somewhere. I pounded on it several times, thinking if Bess and Dave were on the other side, they would pound back. But there wasn't any response."

As Nancy ran forward, her foot kicked a hard object. She stopped and shone her flashlight on it.

"Oh!" she murmured. "It can't be!"

She leaned down and picked up the object. It was the missing end of the railing and newel to the banister which disappeared so mysteriously into the wall of the entrance hall!

"Ned!" Nancy cried out. "Look at this!"

He hurried back and stared at the piece of wood.

"Do you know what this means?" Nancy asked excitedly.

"No. What?"

"At one time," she replied, "that railing and newel must have gone all the way to the bottom of the stairs."

In the thrill of her discovery, Nancy had momentarily forgotten her reason for being in the tunnel.

"Ned!" Nancy cried out. "Look at this!"

She said quickly, "Solving the mystery of the crooked banister will have to wait. I'll give you a hand with that big door, Ned. I wonder what we'll find."

"Bess and Dave, I hope."

They laid their flashlights on the ground, and both tugged as hard as they could at the stout handle. The door began to give a little.

"Pull harder!" Ned urged.

The next moment the door opened with a rush, sending Nancy and Ned over backward onto the ground!

CHAPTER X

Tom Sleepy Deer

NANCY and Ned picked themselves up. Straight ahead was a stairway that led upward into darkness.

"Bess! Dave!" Nancy shouted. They did not answer.

"Let's go up," Nancy suggested.

Ned beamed his flashlight and went first. Nancy followed. At the top of the stairway they saw another heavy door. Both yanked hard but it would not open.

"Bess! Dave!" Ned called loudly.

This time there was a response. A muffled voice replied, "We're here! Locked in! Let us out!"

"Bess!" Nancy shouted in relief. "Is Dave there too?"

"Yes, I am. Look for a hidden button near the door latch."

Nancy and Ned beamed their flashlights on the

area and searched. At first they could detect nothing, then Nancy said, "This thing that looks like a knot in the wood may be it."

Ned pressed it hard and the door opened.

Bess literally fell into Nancy's arms. "Oh, I was so frightened! Dave and I began to think we would never get out of here."

The couple's prison was the round turret encased with unbreakable glass windows, which did not open.

"We tried every way to signal somebody," Dave said. "Bess had a flashlight and we used that but apparently nobody noticed it. Finally the battery went dead."

The four friends descended the stairway, each one asking questions about the trap door.

Bess replied first. "That robot was in the kitchen when we went in. Dave was curious about Robby, so we walked directly toward him. Suddenly he began to make that spooky whirring sound and the next thing we knew the floor under our feet opened and down we went."

Dave took up the story. "Then the trap door shut. I found a box to stand on and tried my best to get the old thing open. But that was hopeless. I pounded on the door but it has some kind of covering that deadens sound. It was impossible to make you hear us."

Bess said, "We decided to investigate the tunnel. Dave and I thought maybe there was an opening to the outdoors at the far end of it. But all we found were the steps leading upward."

Dave told Nancy and Ned that both the lower door to the stairway and the one at the top had swung shut behind the couple.

Bess shuddered. "Maybe we weren't Rawley Banister's first prisoners! It gives me goosebumps to think about it."

When they reached the foot of the stairs, Nancy picked up the piece of railing and newel.

"What's that?" Bess asked.

Nancy told her to take a good look. Bess gasped upon realizing that it was part of the hallway banister.

"You found this down here?" she queried.

"Yes. Do you all realize what this means?"

"One of two things," Ned replied. "Either the piece of railing and newel was sawed off before the staircase was installed, or else it was removed later."

"But why would it have been removed?" Dave asked. "If the builder knew that the one banister was going to end at the wall three feet above the floor, why would he have built it and thrown the piece away?"

Nancy chuckled. "That's another part of the mystery I'll have to solve. And if I do," she added, "I'm sure it will tell us a great deal about Rawley Banister, his swindling operation, and perhaps where he is."

Bess and Dave asked how Nancy and Ned had discovered the trap door. "Did you fall through?" Bess queried.

"No," Nancy replied, and explained what had happened.

They were now below the opening to the kitchen and one by one the four swung themselves up with some assistance from George.

"You're okay!" she cried. "No need to tell you how glad I am to see you. Where were you?"

As Bess and Dave related their harrowing experience, a clock in Mountainville tolled the hour of midnight.

"We'd better go back to the motel," Nancy suggested, looking at Bess who seemed very weary.

Dave grinned. "I could use a little sleep myself," he said.

Nancy took the piece of banister with her. An idea for tracking down this clue was formulating in her mind.

The trap door was closed by hand and Robby was locked in the closet. Nancy hid the key, then the five went to the front of the house. The young detective paused a few moments to compare the newel of the sawed-off banister with the other post. The pieces matched exactly, except that the railings curved in opposite directions.

The lights were extinguished and the front

door locked. Nancy put the key in her handbag.

Burt called out, "So you finally made it back! I sure was worried about you but I didn't dare leave this sapling bridge. By the way, I've been trying to find out what happened to the regular bridge. It's too dark to see much. But I have a good idea that it's down in the water."

After the three couples had crossed the moat Ned suggested that they hide the saplings in the woods. This was done, then Ned slid behind the wheel of his car while the others climbed in.

By the time they reached the foot of the hill, Bess was her usual self, "I'm ready for a midnight snack," she said. "How about the rest of you?"

All admitted they were hungry and were glad to find the motel soda shop still open. Finally good nights were said.

When Nancy, Bess, and George came into the lobby the next morning, the boys were waiting. Bess glanced at the girls' mailbox. There was an envelope in it.

"I wonder whom that's for," she thought as she asked the clerk to hand it to her.

She was surprised to find the letter was addressed to her. It bore an airmail stamp and Arizona postmark. "I don't know anybody out there," she said to herself.

Bess waited to open it until the group was seated for breakfast and had given their orders.

Then she excused herself, slit the envelope, and began to read the letter. Within seconds a broad smile spread over her face.

She looked up and said, "Well, you doubters, now I have proof!"

"Proof of what?" George asked.

Bess flushed slightly. "You remember Clyde Mead. He wanted money to help Indian children. I knew you girls wouldn't approve, so I didn't tell you, but I gave him some."

"Oh, Bess, you didn't!" George cried disapprovingly. "Why—?"

Bess held up her hand. "Don't scold me," she said. "This time you're wrong. Here is a darling letter from a little Indian boy named Tom Sleepy Deer Smith. He received the money I sent and is very happy to use it for his education. So you see, girls, Mr. Clyde Mead was on the up-and-up all the time."

After glancing at the letter, her friends had to admit it was convincing. Nevertheless, Nancy and George could not shake off their suspicions about Clyde Mead.

Bess was hurt. "I can see you don't fully believe all this is true."

Ned spoke up. "Oh, I'm all for helping Indian children who need it."

The others began to question Bess about Clyde Mead's conversation with her. She answered them somberly but could not be convinced that she might have done something unwise.

"To whom did you pay this money?" George asked.

"Mr. Mead."

George frowned. "I'd like to bet the money's in his pocket and not Sleepy Deer's."

Nancy thought it was time to call a truce. She said, "Let's not condemn the man until we can prove he is dishonest."

"I agree," said Ned. "Here comes our food. Let's eat!"

Everyone except Bess seemed to be very hungry and the basket of rolls was passed around three times. Bess merely picked at her food.

Ned felt sorry for her and changed the conversation to a jocular vein. "Bess," he said, "did you ever hear about the girl who went into the luggage store to buy a gift for her fiancé?"

"No."

Grinning, Ned said, "The clerk asked her if she would like a two-suiter. Her reply was, 'No, thank you. One suitor is enough for me. What do you have for just one man?' "

Bess giggled and Burt said, "You have me all confused. Was the girl asking for two suits for one man or one man with two suits?"

The joking continued and soon Bess was feeling cheerful.

Later, as the group walked out of the dining

room, Nancy said to Ned, "This Clyde Mead claimed that he once taught at Emerson College."

Ned shrugged. "It must have been before I enrolled there. But I'll find out for you."

The boys said they must leave immediately. They went for their luggage, then drove off.

After they had gone, Nancy told the other girls she wanted to call on a carpenter and ask him about the piece of banister and newel she had found in the tunnel.

"But first I'll phone Mrs. Carrier and get her okay to show it to a carpenter."

When the woman answered, she was amazed to hear of the young people's adventure the previous night. Worriedly she asked:

"Nancy, are you sure you ought to continue working on this case?"

"Oh yes," Nancy replied, "And I'd like your permission to show the piece of banister to a carpenter."

"Do it by all means," Mrs. Carrier answered. "I recommend Mr. Hurley on Tuttle Street. He's not only a carpenter, but also an excellent woodworker. I'm sure that he'll be able to answer whatever questions you have."

On the way to Mr. Hurley's shop, Bess said to Nancy, "What do you hope to learn from the man?"

"I want to find out, if possible, whether the

banister piece was sawed off before or after the staircase was installed."

"Do you think he can really tell this?" Bess queried.

"If he's a woodworker, I'm sure he can."

When they reached Tuttle Street, Nancy parked the car and the three girls hurried into Mr. Hurley's shop. The place was immaculate. Interesting pieces of wooden statuary and furniture were on display. The owner was seated at a workbench in the rear. He rose and walked forward.

"Can I help you?" he asked.

Nancy told him why she was there. She pulled the piece of banister from her large shopping bag and handed it to him.

Mr. Hurley took the wood, then cried out, "Where did you get this?"

CHAPTER XI

Important Clue

For a second Nancy was tempted to tell Mr. Hurley where the piece of banister and newel had come from. But she decided against this and merely answered, "I found it in a cellar, and wondered why it had been sawed off."

The carpenter smiled. "For a moment I thought it was like one I saw in a photograph. It might have been removed because it was not perfect. Perhaps it did not match the opposite one on the staircase."

Nancy was tempted to say, "Oh yes it does." Instead she asked, "Can you tell me how long ago this was sawed off?"

"Possibly," Mr. Hurley replied. Using a magnifying glass, he studied the mahogany rail and post.

Nancy, Bess, and George exchanged excited glances. By this time the cousins had guessed what was going through Nancy's mind and could hardly wait for the carpenter to tell them his conclusion.

Finally he replied. "I'd say from the color of the raw wood this piece was sawed off about three years ago."

Nancy was excited. Her hunch had been correct. The wall into which the short side of the banister ran had been put up a good many years after the house was built. According to Mrs. Carrier, Rawley had had his home constructed ten years ago!

"Why, oh why, was that extra wall added?" Nancy asked herself over and over.

Suddenly it occurred to her that Mr. Hurley could be wrong. She had better not jump to any conclusion until she had more proof.

Taking the wood piece from the carpenter, she said, "It was Mrs. Carrier who suggested I come to you. Have you ever been to her brother Rawley's house?"

"No, I haven't. But I understand it's a pretty kooky place."

Nancy thanked Mr. Hurley for his help and was about to leave with her friends when the man said, "Wait a minute! I just recalled something. A friend of mine worked in that house. He's the one who told me it's crazy and showed me pictures of it. He'd be glad to tell you about the place, I'm sure. Why don't you go to see him?"

"That would be interesting," Nancy replied. "Where is his shop?"

"Over in the town of Charlotte. He's easy to find. Right on Main Street. Number 27. His name is Custer—Hugo Custer."

Nancy told Mr. Hurley she appreciated the information and the three girls said good-by. On the way to Charlotte they discussed Nancy's clue about a new wall built by Rawley.

"I hope," Bess said, "that you have no idea of tearing down what you think is a false wall. Why, there could be lots of dangerous things behind there!"

"Like what?" George asked her.

Bess replied that she could imagine all kinds of things. "Snakes and—"

George made a face at her cousin. "There are times, Bess, when you come up with the most ghastly ideas. How could snakes possibly live cooped up in a wall with nothing to eat or drink?"

Bess was not to be dissuaded. "They could go down through the floor and to the outdoors. Okay, George, what do you think might be behind that wall?"

"Something fabulous, like a great treasure," she quickly replied.

Bess disagreed. "If that were true, when Rawley Banister was caught, why didn't he sell the treasure and pay off his debts and bail?"

" 'Cause he's a crook," George said flatly.

Nancy interrupted the argument by saying she thought they had missed the sign to Charlotte. "I'm going to turn around. Girls, please keep your eyes open."

She had not gone far in the opposite direction before Bess spotted a small sign with an arrow which pointed to Charlotte. Nancy turned onto the road and ten minutes later drove into the little village.

They found Hugo Custer's shop without any trouble. Fortunately the carpenter was there and welcomed his callers warmly.

"Your friend Mr. Hurley suggested that we come to see you," Nancy said. "We're curious about the Banister house. He said that you have worked there."

The carpenter nodded. "I put an extra closet in Mr. Banister's bedroom. That house sure is crazy."

"How long ago did you work there?" Nancy queried.

"Let me see. It must have been five years or more."

Nancy's pulse quickened. She wondered what question to ask next, but Mr. Custer went on, "If you want to get inside, I'm afraid I can't be of any help. Rawley Banister has disappeared. I believe he jumped bail. Too bad he got into trouble. Banister was a talented young man, but he should have known he couldn't break the law and get away with it forever."

"That's right," George spoke up. "Nancy's father is a lawyer so we hear a great deal about such people."

Mr. Custer proved to be an exceptionally talkative person. The girls asked a few more questions.

"Of all the crazily built things in Mr. Banister's house," he said, "the one that took the prize was the staircase in the center of the big entrance hall. From top to bottom there were hardly two steps in a row that were at the same angle. The whole thing zigzagged—crookedest, craziest thing I've ever seen. But you know it was funny. The lower end of it was very graceful and normal."

Nancy, Bess, and George leaned forward to hear more. As the carpenter paused, Nancy asked, "Normal in what way?"

"Well, the banisters ended in very graceful newels and the two bottom steps were just like any regular ones."

"Did Rawley Banister tell you why he'd had the staircase built that way?" Nancy queried.

Mr. Custer said no. "Mr. Banister didn't talk much and left me alone most of the time. I certainly didn't get the impression he was queer or abnormal. But I guess he must have been, building his house the way he did. I've quite a few pictures of it. Would you like to see them?"

"Oh yes," Nancy answered.

While the carpenter looked through some drawers in an old-fashioned desk, he kept talking about the zigzag house. "I'd seen it from the outside, so when Mr. Banister asked me to come, I took along my camera and some flashbulbs. If I found things as strange inside as I had outside, I was going to take pictures."

Nancy glanced at her friends and George gave her a big wink. She whispered, "This is your lucky day!"

By this time Mr. Custer had found the pictures. He laid them on a table and explained each one. Everything was familiar to the girls except the entrance hall. Bess could not suppress a gasp of surprise.

The carpenter grinned. "I thought that would give you a start," he said. "I'll bet there isn't another staircase like that one."

"No, I guess not," Bess answered.

The three girls studied the pictures carefully. The staircase was directly in the center of the large hall and showed the full banisters and the two newels! Here was proof that some time during the past five years Rawley had built the extra wall.

"I can see you're really intrigued by these snapshots," Mr. Custer said. "I have a few duplicates. Would you like some?"

"Indeed I would," Nancy replied. "This is very kind of you, Mr. Custer. Will you let me pay for the prints?"

"No, no. I'm happy to give them to you." The man's eyes twinkled. "It isn't often that three attractive young ladies come into my shop. We'll call the pictures a souvenir of your visit."

"I'm very grateful," Nancy told him.

The girls lingered a short while, hoping Mr. Custer might give them more clues, but in a few minutes they realized he had told them all he knew. They expressed their appreciation for his help and left.

Nancy looked very happy over the outcome of her visit. "Now all my suspicions are confirmed," she said. "I can hardly wait to get back to Rawley's house."

"Let's not go now," Bess suggested. "It's way past lunchtime and I'm starved."

The girls ate in an attractive motel restaurant, then started for Mountainville.

Presently Nancy said, "I think we should tell Mrs. Carrier what we learned and show her these pictures."

George remarked, "You have to return the key anyway."

During the drive the girls talked about Rawley Banister and his weird ideas.

"Do you think he might turn up again at his home?" Bess asked.

George answered, "I doubt it! He's probably too busy gypping people in faraway places."

When Mrs. Carrier opened her door, she exclaimed, "Why, girls, how glad I am to see you!"

She kissed each one and led the way into her living room.

"How is the case going?" she asked.

The girls took turns telling about their interesting adventure that day and Nancy showed the snapshots of Rawley's house.

When Mrs. Carrier saw the picture of the entrance hall, she exclaimed, "How extraordinary! Well, if Rawley doesn't show up in a reasonable length of time, I believe we should investigate behind that new wall."

Then abruptly she changed the subject. "Guess who was here this morning?"

"Your brother Thomas?" Bess questioned.

"No. Guess again."

"My dad?" Nancy asked.

"No. Give another guess."

George spoke up. "Ned and Burt and Dave?"

Mrs. Carrier shook her head and Nancy said, "I give up."

"So do I," said Bess and George.

"Well, you're in for a big surprise. Mr. Clyde Mead came to call."

CHAPTER XII

Phony Membership

"CLYDE Mead was here?" Bess asked Mrs. Carrier in surprise. "You mean the one who is interested in Indian children?"

Mrs. Carrier smiled. "He's the one. Said he knows you. A very attractive man. We had a lovely talk."

Nancy and George looked at each other but made no comment.

Bess asked, "Did he tell you about the Indian children he's trying to help?"

"Indeed he did. Mr. Mead said you had been kind enough to assist one of them."

Bess's face lighted up. "I even had a letter from the little boy. His name is Tom Sleepy Deer Smith."

She took the letter from her handbag and gave it to Mrs. Carrier. As the woman read it, a pleased expression came over her face.

"If I needed any proof that Mr. Mead's story was on the level, this is it."

Bess asked if she too had agreed to help an Indian child.

"Yes, I did," Mrs. Carrier replied. "A darling little girl. Mr. Mead said she will write to me after she receives my donation."

Once more Nancy and George looked at each other. They were still suspicious about Mr. Mead's project. However, if Mrs. Carrier did receive a letter, perhaps it would prove that their doubts were unfounded.

Nancy finally spoke up. "Mrs. Carrier, did you make out a check to Mr. Mead to be forwarded to the Indians?"

"Why yes. Don't you think that was all right?"

Bess answered, "Of course it was. You know, Mrs. Carrier, Nancy and George didn't like Mr. Mead from the moment they met him and I'm afraid they don't quite trust him."

Bess wore a smug expression, mixed with a smile.

George remarked, "Frankly we didn't. I certainly hope, Mrs. Carrier, that your money will get to the Indian child and not go into Mr. Mead's pocket."

"What do you mean?" the woman cried out in alarm.

George gave a candid answer. "The letters from the Indian children could be fakes."

"Oh my goodness!" Mrs. Carrier exclaimed. "I never thought of that. I see what you mean. This Mr. Mead could have a partner in Arizona who sends these letters whenever he's requested to."

"Exactly," George replied.

Nancy turned the conversation to Rawley's house. "I can hardly wait to investigate that wall with the serpent picture."

"But, girls, please don't go there by yourselves," Mrs. Carrier requested. "I finally found a man who is willing to guard the place. He'll patrol the grounds.

"But this won't make it any safer indoors. I don't want you falling through any more trap doors or getting locked in towers or having that robot attack you again."

Nancy was disappointed. She must figure out a way to get into the house without disregarding Mrs. Carrier's request.

The doorbell rang and Mrs. Carrier went to answer it. She returned shortly, followed by her brother Thomas and a couple. She introduced them to the girls as Mr. and Mrs. Jacques.

"You may speak freely in front of these young ladies," Mrs. Carrier went on. "They are trying to help us find my brother Rawley."

Mrs. Jacques stared at the girls. She had a hard, unpleasant face. Her flashy clothes and hairdo were not in good taste.

"I was never so humiliated in all my life!" she said. "We were actually turned away from the Mountain Ridge Country Club after my husband had paid a lot of money to get in!"

"I don't understand," Mrs. Carrier said.

Mr. Jacques, a thin, sharp-eyed man with a small mustache and a tiny goatee, took up the story.

"Your brother Rawley offered to get us membership in the club. Knowing your family's fine reputation in the neighborhood, my wife and I had no idea the whole thing would turn out to be a fraud."

"A fraud!" Mrs. Carrier cried out.

"That's what I said—a fraud," Mr. Jacques told her. His face was becoming red with anger. "Your brother Rawley swindled us out of a good bit of money and I am determined to get it back!"

Thomas interrupted. "Suppose you tell my sister and the girls exactly what happened."

Mr. Jacques said, "We knew there was a long waiting list, but your brother approached us, saying he could get us membership right away. He wouldn't explain how he was going to do it, but we assumed of course it was family influence."

His wife, looking disdainfully at everyone, added, "Rawley Banister gave us an application to fill out. He told us it would be necessary to pay an initiation fee in advance and also a good-sized bonus in order to put our names ahead of everyone else's."

Nancy spoke up. "Were you ever given a membership card?"

"Oh yes," Mrs. Jacques replied. "Then one evening, when there was going to be a dance at the club, we got dressed up and went there. The man at the door did not recognize us and asked to see our membership card. My husband showed it to him."

"Then what happened?" George asked eagerly.

Mr. Jacques said he and his wife had been asked to sit down in the hallway. "The president of the club came out. When he saw our membership card, he told us it was a fake. Of course I became angry, so he pulled his own card from a pocket. It was totally different from the one I held."

Mrs. Jacques burst out, "It was positively insulting the way we were treated. We had to stay in the hall until the chairman of the membership committee came out. He had never heard of us, and our names had never been brought up at any meetings. We were politely but firmly asked to leave."

Mrs. Carrier was blushing in embarrassment. She was speechless as Mr. Jacques went on to tell that he had threatened to sue the club.

"And I'm not sure I won't still do that very thing," he added.

At first Nancy had felt sorry for the couple. But now her sympathy vanished. These people had tried to push their way into the club and had even paid a bonus for the privilege!

She said quietly, "Mr. Jacques, are you sure you have a case? The country club didn't swindle you."

"But Rawley Banister is a club member," the man retorted. He stood up. "Come on, Millie," he said to his wife. "I thought these people would have enough family pride to pay us their brother's debt, but I can see they don't."

Mrs. Carrier said, "Rawley will be home soon, I'm sure. We'll see that he contacts you."

Both Mr. and Mrs. Jacques laughed sarcastically and the man said, "You'll never see that crooked brother of yours again! I'm sure he's skipped out for good!"

With that the irate man stomped from the living room, followed by his wife. The couple hurried out the front door and drove away. Tears came into Mrs. Carrier's eyes and Thomas looked very sober.

Nancy tried to cheer them up by saying, "The Jacques didn't give us any proof that they had paid out a nickel. Please don't worry. In the meantime, let me call my father. He can advise us."

"Please do that," Mrs. Carrier said.

Mr. Drew was delighted to hear from Nancy since he had news for her too. "But first, tell me why you called."

When he heard about the Jacques being swindled out of membership in the country club, he said that Mrs. Carrier and her brother Thomas had nothing to worry about. The Jacques could sue neither them nor the country club. They had been the victims of a con man and if they ever got their money back they would be lucky.

"Mrs. Carrier and Thomas feel pretty bad about Rawley's actions. And now, tell me your news."

The lawyer said he too had been trying to trace Rawley Banister. "I finally had some luck. I learned that he recently purchased a high-powered cruiser in Miami."

"That's great news!" Nancy exclaimed. "Where is he now?"

Mr. Drew said that unfortunately nobody knew. "Rawley took off for parts unknown. But every port along the Atlantic Coast, including those in the Caribbean Islands, has been alerted. If he shows up, which he'll have to do to buy fuel, he'll be arrested."

"That's a terrific lead!" said Nancy.

She told her father about having seen pictures

of the center hall of Rawley's house before the new wall had been put up. The lawyer was amazed.

"Dad," she said, "I strongly suspect something of value is hidden behind that wall. Mrs. Carrier doesn't want us girls to be in the house alone. Do you think you could possibly come up here for a little while and do some investigating with us?"

"Certainly," her father replied. He chuckled. "Will tomorrow morning be soon enough?"

"Oh, Dad, you're the greatest!"

"Okay, I'll drive up to the motel and have breakfast with you girls."

Nancy went back to the living room and reported what her father had said. Mrs. Carrier and Thomas were amazed to hear about Rawley. They were glad to learn that Mr. Drew was coming to Mountainville the next day.

"I'd like to go out to Rawley's house with you," Mrs. Carrier said eagerly.

"We'll pick you up at ten o'clock," Nancy promised. "How about you, Thomas? Would you like to come?"

"Sorry, but I have a business appointment."

Mrs. Carrier invited the girls to stay for dinner. Shortly after nine o'clock they returned to the motel. There was a letter in the girls' mailbox. As the clerk handed it to Nancy, he remarked, "As you see, there's no stamp or return name or address on this. I found it lying on the counter."

Nancy took the envelope and stared at it. Her name had been typed on.

The girls hurried to their room. When they were inside, Nancy tore open the envelope.

The contents had also been typed and were brief.

The note said:

Hunt for the Skeleton's Bracelet

CHAPTER XIII

Strange Portraits

"O-OH, how creepy!" Bess exclaimed as she re-read the mysterious note. " 'Hunt for the Skeleton's Bracelet!' "

Nancy and George were equally amazed and agreed with Bess that it sounded pretty gruesome. Nancy held up the sheet of paper and the envelope to the light, hoping to find watermarks or other clues to the sender.

"There are none," she reported.

"Do you suppose," George said, "that this could be a joke of some kind?"

"How could it be?" Bess asked.

George said there were many people around who knew that Nancy Drew was an amateur detective. "Somebody could have figured it would be funny to send her a message like this."

The cousins asked Nancy what she thought.

"I'm inclined to think there is real meaning in

the note," she replied. "Pranksters usually sign their notes with some funny name. In this case it could have been Old Bones." The other girls laughed.

Bess asked, "But where would the skeleton or the bracelet be?"

"I have a strong hunch," Nancy replied, "that the answer is in Rawley Banister's house."

George suggested, "Perhaps the bracelet is hidden behind that new wall."

Nancy went to the phone. "I'm going to call Mrs. Carrier and see if she can give us a clue."

The woman was as mystified as Nancy. "But I don't think the note is a hoax," she said. "A skeleton's bracelet sounds exactly like what my brother might have purchased at some time and hidden away."

"Have you any idea who might have written the note?" Nancy asked.

"No, but I doubt that it was Rawley. According to your father, he's far away from here."

After Nancy had said good-by, the girls continued to talk about the mysterious piece of jewelry.

"Maybe," Bess suggested, "we'll find a skeleton with a priceless bracelet dangling from his or her wrist."

George grinned. "I'll bet the bracelet was stolen from the arm of a person deceased in ancient times. A queen, maybe."

Nancy began to undress. "Listen, girls, if you don't stop talking about such morbid things, you're likely to have bad dreams and not sleep well. We want to be alert for tomorrow's sleuthing in Rawley's house."

The girls began talking of more pleasant subjects. Half an hour later all of them were sound asleep. None had a bad dream.

The following morning when they entered the motel restaurant for breakfast Mr. Drew was waiting for them. Nancy rushed over to kiss him, followed by Bess and George.

After they had given the waitress their orders, Mr. Drew said, "I hope you all had a good night with no scares or no new mysteries popping up."

The girls grinned and George said, "You wouldn't expect Nancy to go that many hours without stumbling upon a new mystery, would you?"

Mr. Drew looked at his daughter. "Now what's up?"

Nancy pulled the strange note from her handbag and gave it to him.

"Hm!" he said. "This is certainly something different. Nancy, I suppose you have the mystery half solved by now. What's your theory about the note?"

She laughed and told him Bess's guess that in Rawley's house they would find a hidden skeleton wearing a jeweled bracelet.

Mr. Drew grinned at Bess but admitted that it was possible. "I imagine what you have in mind is the area behind that new wall in the hall."

Bess nodded.

Nancy asked her father his opinion of the anonymous note.

He answered, "Anonymous notes are usually the work of cowards. There are times, particularly during a war or a tight dictatorship, when anonymous notes are written to protect the life of the sender. But what we sometimes call crank letters, or warning notes, are sent without a signature because the writer is too cowardly to voice his opinion openly."

Shortly before ten o'clock the foursome set off in Nancy's car. They called for Mrs. Carrier, then drove directly to Rawley's house.

As they pulled into the parking area near the moat, Bess exclaimed, "Nancy, the bridge is in place again! I hope it stays there."

An idea for the group's safety occurred to Nancy and she said, "I think we had better carry those saplings to the other side of the bridge in case it should suddenly disappear again."

"A sound idea," her father agreed. "It's evident a mischief-maker other than Rawley is involved in some of the things going on here. If Rawley is off in the Caribbean on his fast cruiser, he couldn't possibly have made this bridge vanish and reappear."

"Or have left the mysterious note at the motel," his daughter added.

"Maybe it's that man we saw running away from here the other night," George suggested.

Nancy nodded. "And who can he be? Rawley's ruled out—that's definite."

Mr. Drew and the girls retrieved the saplings from their hiding place and transported them across the bridge. On the other side they were met by the guard, who asked why they were carrying the young trees. Mrs. Carrier explained.

"I see," the guard said. "The bridge was in place when I arrived this morning." He introduced himself as Les Morton. "If you folks are going to be here a while, I'd like to take off a little time. Okay if I'm back in an hour?"

"That will be all right," Mrs. Carrier answered. She looked at the saplings. "Do you suppose they'll be safe here? I'd hate to have anyone take them and leave us stranded."

"I'll show you where to hide them," the guard said. "Around back there's a pile of brush. How about putting the saplings under it?"

He helped carry the young trees to the spot, then left. The others went into the house.

"Where shall we start?" Bess asked.

Mr. Drew walked up the crooked staircase to look around. Nancy said she was going to concentrate on the banister and glanced at the snapshot the carpenter had given her. Then, holding up the sawed-off piece of banister and newel, she found that it would have reached about two feet inside the mysterious wall. Next she went into the living room and studied the bookcase which reached from the ceiling to the floor.

"Got a clue?" George queried.

"I think so," Nancy replied. "This bookcase is rounded. Perhaps it swivels. By taking down the original wall and putting up the new one, there was room for this piece to revolve."

George gave the bookcase a yank but it did not budge. "There must be a hidden spring," she said.

Nancy was already examining the wall on either side but could find no button, lever, or secret panel.

As she stood looking thoughtfully into space, George remarked, "I guess we're stymied."

Bess, who had been scanning the many volumes in the twelve-foot-wide bookcase, commented, "Rawley must have been a great reader."

"He was," his sister agreed. "But he leaned toward bizarre subjects."

Suddenly Bess gave a little squeal. "Here's a book that might be a clue to something!"

Taking it out, she held up the volume which told about the anatomy of the human body. The cover displayed a skeleton.

"But he isn't wearing a bracelet," George commented.

Nancy went to the spot from which Bess had taken the book. She removed several volumes near it and looked intently at the board in back of the shelf.

"I think I see something!" she said excitedly.

"What is it?" asked Mrs. Carrier.

Nancy was pushing a secret panel aside. Beyond she could faintly see balance weights. Gingerly she touched one of them.

Almost instantly the bookcase began to revolve.

Mrs. Carrier and the girls jumped back and waited to see what was on the other side. To their utter astonishment there were no bookshelves. Instead, on the rounded wall hung more than a dozen gold-framed portraits.

"All the faces have been blacked out!" Bess exclaimed, staring at the oil paintings.

Mrs. Carrier gave a cry of dismay. At the same time the girls noticed that there were nameplates on the paintings. Some portraits were of men, others of women, but all were named Banister.

"How weird!" Bess murmured, shrinking back from the damaged portraits. "Why would anybody want to do such a thing?"

"I can answer that," Mrs. Carrier replied. "My brother Rawley hated those relatives. But how mean of him to destroy their lovely faces! The Banisters were very handsome and intelligent-looking."

Meanwhile Mr. Drew had been examining the

new wall from top to bottom. He went back to the second floor to make an experiment. He had found a slight crack between the wall and the ceiling above and now shoved a twenty-five-cent piece through it. He listened intently to detect a thud but just at this moment the exclamations from the living room drowned out any other sound.

Mr. Drew rushed down the crooked staircase and dashed into the living room. He stopped short and gazed in astonishment at the sight before him.

"What a find!" he exclaimed. "But why would anyone mar the paintings in that way?"

Again Mrs. Carrier spoke of her brother's hatred for those members of the family.

Mr. Drew looked at the portraits closely. "Nancy, do you think there might be a clue under the blotted-out faces?"

George, curious, tried to see what lay beyond the bookcase. "Nancy, lend me your flashlight."

She beamed the light into the fractional opening on either side but could detect nothing. Just then Bess noticed that the bookcase was starting to revolve again.

"Look out!" she shouted at her cousin.

George just avoided being squeezed but could not pull Nancy's flashlight away in time. It went on around with the bookcase and they heard it fall to the floor. She apologized for its loss.

"All their faces have been blacked out!" Bess exclaimed

"Maybe it was a good thing," Mr. Drew remarked. "At least we know there's a floor in the area beyond."

Nancy glanced up at her father and grinned. "Meaning that when we get in there, we'll have something to stand on." He smiled and nodded.

The bookcase had revolved to its usual position and stopped. When Mr. Drew said he wanted to examine the portraits, Nancy reached in through the sliding panel and touched the weight. The bookcase did not move. She pulled the counterbalance. Still nothing happened.

"Oh dear!" she exclaimed. "I must have broken the mechanism!"

George stood surveying the shelves. "Maybe," she said, "if I take out a lot of the books, I could lie down on the shelf and ride around to the other side. Then I can tell you what's there."

Her hopes were dashed, however, because although they all pulled and tugged, they could not budge the bookcase.

Bess sighed. "Maybe we ruined everything!"

CHAPTER XIV

A Weird Story

Mrs. Carrier, still angry over the blotted-out faces of her relatives, said bitterly, "I think such destruction is unforgivable. This is Rawley's home to be sure, but there are certain things that go beyond all reason."

She went on, "If my brother Rawley isn't found soon, I declare I'm going to have this whole bookcase torn down. Then we can get at those pictures. I hope that whatever paint was used to cover the faces can be removed easily."

Nancy put an arm around the irate woman. "I'm sure the pictures can be restored," she said. "Art shops do wonderful things these days."

Thinking it might calm Mrs. Carrier to get away from the bookcase, she said, "My dad didn't have much time to see the house on his first visit. Wouldn't you like to show him around? I'll go with you."

The three toured both floors, while Bess and

George continued to work on the bookcase. Mr. Drew studied the unusual designs in the carved woodwork. By the time they returned to the first floor, Mrs. Carrier seemed to be her usual self.

She even laughed and said cheerily, "Mr. Drew, tell me, have you ever heard of such a crazy place?"

The lawyer smiled. "I can't say I have. I imagine, though, that your brother had a lot of fun building this house. It's amazing to me why he never invited any relatives here. Surely they would have been highly entertained."

Mrs. Carrier said she could not understand this either. "As far as we know now, his only companion was a robot."

"I would prefer a human servant at any time!" Mr. Drew remarked.

Just then Bess called excitedly, "Everybody come here at once! Quick!"

The three hurried to the living room. Bess and George were poring over a volume they had found in the bookcase. Nancy asked what the title was and George replied, "It's called *Archaeological Finds in Jewelry*. Take a look at this page."

The open book revealed the picture of a gold bracelet made of intertwined serpents. Each one had a ruby eye, and the jewel piece was encrusted with turquoise. Nancy noticed that the page had been marked in ink with a large asterisk.

Bess cried out, "This must be the skeleton's bracelet! Here it says the ancient bracelet was found on the bony arm of an unknown Aztec woman's skeleton!"

George began to read the text aloud:

" 'Mystery shrouds the identity of the woman who wore the bracelet. During a dig in a lonely area far away from cities, the skeleton was found intact. It is thought that the woman died from the venom of a poisonous snake. Whether the bracelet was hers or was put on after her death is not known.' "

"Listen to this!" Bess burst out as George paused. "It says here that the skeleton and the bracelet disappeared mysteriously from the dig. The thief probably sold them, but there is no record as to where they went."

The girls looked at one another. Each was thinking the same thing. Had Rawley Banister purchased the skeleton and bracelet from the thief? In deference to Mrs. Carrier, they did not express the thought aloud.

"You won't mind if I go outdoors for a little while?" she asked. "This place is making me nervous. Some fresh air will do me good."

Mr. Drew asked if she would like to go home, but Mrs. Carrier insisted that he and the girls go on with their investigation.

"I'll feel better in a little while," she assured them.

As soon as she had gone outside, the others discussed the anonymous note Nancy had received and its relation to the story in the book.

"One thing is sure," said George. "Somebody who knows about the bracelet hasn't found it yet. He wants Nancy to do this for him."

"You could be right," Mr. Drew replied. "Then, after Nancy finds the bracelet, he'll try to steal it."

Bess asked, "Do you think the writer of the note knows the bracelet is here? Has he been trying to locate it, but failed?"

The others shrugged, and George said, "Anything's possible."

Nancy reminded her friends that unless they started a search for the bracelet, none of them would ever find it.

"I think the location of this book in the shelves may be a clue. Where was it?" she asked.

Bess pointed to a space between other volumes. Nancy quickly took out the books near that spot, then examined the rear wooden panel. There was no sign of another opening or any hidden contrivance.

"I suggest," said Mr. Drew, "that we take every book out of the case. We might be able to discover some way to make the piece revolve again."

The books were removed an armful at a time and put in consecutive piles so they could be correctly restored to their original positions. The eyes of the three girls and Mr. Drew swept over the entire surface of the backing from ceiling to floor.

Finally Nancy remarked, "I guess the sliding secret panel is the only way to make this thing revolve."

Again she put her hand into the opening and felt all around the weights. Her fingers touched a small lever. The instant she moved it, the sliding panel slammed shut onto her wrist.

"Ouch!" she cried out and tried with her other hand to pull the panel back. It would not give an inch.

The next second the bookcase began to revolve. Nancy tried frantically to release her injured hand.

"Help!" she cried.

Mr. Drew jumped forward. Calling to Bess and George to help him, he held onto the bookcase. With their combined strength, they managed to keep it from revolving farther.

Nancy's hand was numb by this time. Desperately she tried to find some mechanism so she could free herself.

"It's no use!" Nancy thought. But the determined girl grit her teeth and said aloud, "Somebody hand me a heavy book."

Bess picked one up. Nancy took it in her left hand and swung the volume with all her might against the sliding panel. The wood shivered but did not give way. She gave it another hard whack. This time there was a splintering sound and a piece of the panel fell down behind the partition. Quickly Nancy pulled out her hand.

Mr. Drew and the girls let go of the bookcase, which once more began to revolve. They heaved sighs of relief.

"You had a narrow escape!" Bess said sympathetically. "Your whole hand might have been ripped off!"

"Yes, I know," said Nancy. "Thank you all for helping me. I think I'll go and run cold water over my wrist and hand." She went into the kitchen.

Circulation was soon restored and she returned to the living room. By this time Mrs. Carrier had come inside. She was listening to Bess's graphic description of what had happened.

"This place is just too dangerous for you girls to work in," she said dismally.

Nancy tried to cheer up the woman. "We're going to solve this whole mystery soon, I'm sure of it. Please don't worry."

She noticed that the bookcase had swung around to the portrait side. Her father had jammed a wedge into one side so the mechanism could not work.

"I think we should examine each of these pictures," he said. "One or more of them may contain a clue."

He lifted down five of the portraits and handed one to each person in the room. There was complete quiet for a few minutes as they all scanned the pictures carefully.

Suddenly Mrs. Carrier cried out, "This face! There's money under the black paint!"

She started chipping off the black coating with her fingernails. The others crowded around to watch.

Two minutes later Mrs. Carrier pulled her hand away from the portrait, grabbed her fingers, and cried out in pain!

CHAPTER XV

Nancy's Stratagem

At Mrs. Carrier's outcry, Mr. Drew's face took on a look of alarm. "Nancy," he said, "do you have your magnifying glass with you?"

"Yes, I do," she replied and went for her handbag.

Mr. Drew examined the paint which Mrs. Carrier had been scraping with her fingernails.

"I need a knife," he said, and Nancy hurried to the kitchen to get one.

Her father chipped off more of the paint, then exclaimed, "The face on this portrait is covered with steel nails that are holding down a thousand-dollar bill."

Suddenly Mrs. Carrier said, "I believe they're more than plain steel nails. See how my hand is swelling."

The others looked at her in alarm. Bess cried out, "I'll bet there's poison on them!"

"I believe you're right," said Mr. Drew. "I

think I'd better take Mrs. Carrier to a doctor at once."

"The hospital is closer," the woman said. She was beginning to scratch herself with her uninjured hand. "I itch all over," she complained.

Mr. Drew said that either the paint was poisonous or the steel nails fastened to the portrait had been brushed with poison. "Come, we'll leave right now," he told Mrs. Carrier. "You girls be very careful while I'm gone. I'll return as soon as I can."

As Nancy took a sixth portrait from the wall, Bess said worriedly, "Nancy, don't you dare touch that!"

The young detective smiled. "I'm certainly not going to touch it with my bare hands," she said. "But I think these scrapings of paint and these steel nails should be analyzed by a chemist. He'll be able to tell what kind of poison they contain."

George said she was not afraid to work with Nancy. She procured another knife from the kitchen and also two paper bags. Bess sheepishly followed and returned with a knife and a bag.

The girls worked for a long time in silence. Each one was very careful not to let the paint touch her skin. The shavings were dropped into the bags.

Finally George spoke up. "How are we going to remove the nails without touching them?"

"I saw a tool drawer in the kitchen," Nancy said. "Maybe I can find a pair of pliers."

She soon returned with the tool. One by one Nancy pulled the nails from the picture on which Mrs. Carrier had been working. Most of the black paint had been scraped from the portrait and the girls could distinguish the face beneath.

"Ugh!" Bess exclaimed. "Mrs. Carrier thought all the Banisters were handsome. I guess she forgot this one."

George pointed out that the man had very fine features, but admitted he had a stern, cruel expression.

Bess commented, "I don't blame Rawley Banister for not liking him. He gives me the creeps."

Nancy laughed. "Well, Bess, you won't have to worry about meeting him. I judge from the man's clothes that he lived a long time ago."

"He makes me nervous," Bess insisted. She picked up the portrait and hung it face inward on the wall.

Just then there was loud, persistent rapping of the front-door knocker. "I guess Dad is back," Nancy remarked, and went into the hall.

It occurred to her that this kind of summons did not seem like her father but rather that of an impatient caller.

"I'd better see first who's there before I let anyone in."

Previously she had noticed a peephole in the front door. A person inside the house could look out but no one could peer in. She put one eye to the hole.

Standing outside was a huge man. His face was red and he was pacing back and forth nervously. Not bothering to use the knocker, he banged hard on the door with his fists.

"I don't think I should let him in," Nancy told herself, surmising that he could be unfriendly.

Perhaps the stranger had been watching the place. After he had seen Mr. Drew leave, the man might have concluded he could handle the three girls alone.

"There's no telling what he may be up to," Nancy thought.

She decided to try strategy. Imitating the recorded voice which had greeted her and Mr. Drew on their first visit, she said loud and clear:

"Mr. Banister is not at home. Come back some other time." A couple of seconds later she repeated the message.

Once more she looked through the peephole. The huge man at the door grew even redder in the face and waved his fist.

"Okay," he yelled, "but I'll get him yet! Rawley Banister can't swindle me and not pay for it!"

After delivering his threat, the man walked

away. Taking long steps, he strode across the bridge angrily and headed for a parked car.

Nancy smiled. Her ruse had worked! She returned to the other girls and told them what had happened.

Bess said, "I'm glad you didn't let him in! He sounds like trouble!"

"He sure does!" George agreed. "I wonder who he is."

Nancy shrugged. "Apparently another one of Rawley's victims. He was big enough and mad enough to give the swindler a good beating."

The girls continued their work of uncovering the portrait faces without their fingers touching the surface. Several pictures had thousand-dollar bills secreted under the paint.

"I can't see," said Bess, "why anybody would bother to hide money and then put poison on it. He wouldn't be able to use it."

Nancy suggested that the bills could be washed. Bess and George commented that this was just one more idiosyncrasy of the man who had built the fantastic house. Finally the girls became weary of their task and gave up. They had collected sufficient samples for a chemical analysis.

The front-door knocker sounded again, but less noisily. This time the caller was Mr. Drew. With him was Thomas Banister who seemed very upset over what had taken place.

"This is astounding," he remarked, after greeting the girls. "I can't imagine what ailed my brother. He's a sick man, no doubt about it."

Nancy asked how Mrs. Carrier was. Mr. Drew replied, "She'll be all right, but the doctor said that she had come to the hospital just in the nick of time."

"How dreadful!" Bess exclaimed.

Mr. Drew was told about the paint samples. "Good," he said. "The doctor will want to have these scrapings analyzed. Why don't you girls bring them to him before lunch and see how Mrs. Carrier is feeling?"

Nancy agreed and suggested that perhaps they should release the wedge from the bookcase and let it revolve into place.

Her father nodded. "And we'll return the books to the shelves."

While this was being done, Bess came across a volume entitled *Poisonous Plants, Insects and Snakes*. She sat down and began to turn the pages. She hoped that one would be marked, giving a clue to the poison on the portraits! She looked carefully at each page. Finally near the end of the book, she came across the drawing of a cobra.

"Look, everybody!" Bess called out. "Here's a snake exactly like the one in the wall hanging!"

The others hurried to her side and gazed at the deadly snake.

"Here it states," she went on, "that the venom of the cobra can kill a victim within an hour! Do you suppose the poison on the portraits is from a cobra?"

"Let's look at that serpent picture in the hall," Nancy suggested.

She and the others rushed from the living room and gazed up at the wall hanging which hung directly above the end of the cut-off crooked banister.

Had the searchers stumbled upon a clue?

CHAPTER XVI

Double Suspects

To avoid possible contamination from the Oriental wall hanging, Nancy and her friends used paper towels to lift it down. Gingerly they turned it over.

"I don't see anything suspicious," George remarked.

Nancy took out her magnifying glass and went over every inch of both sides of the serpent picture. "Neither do I," she said finally. "But I wonder if we should take off the back. What do you think, Dad?"

"I think we should leave the piece as it is," he replied. "It would be wiser to solve this mystery in some safer way."

Mr. Drew added that he must return to River Heights directly after lunch. He glanced at his watch. "We'll have to go now."

Nancy locked the front door and pocketed the

key. Les Morton the guard was just returning and apologized for being away longer than he had expected. He helped Nancy and the others carry the saplings back to the woods. Then the group climbed into Mr. Drew's car.

On the way to the hospital Thomas Banister expressed concern that there was still no definite clue to his brother's whereabouts. "The police have an alarm out in every state."

Mr. Drew spoke up. "And as Nancy told you, all ports in the Carribbean Islands have been alerted, but neither Rawley nor his cruiser have been seen in that area."

"I'm greatly worried about Rawley," Thomas Banister said. "He's such a daredevil there's no telling what he may try. This uncertainty is maddening. I wish my brother would return and face the music."

The others did not comment and in a short time arrived at the hospital. They learned that Mrs. Carrier had gone home, so Thomas drove off in his car to see his sister.

Nancy left the poisonous paint flakes with the chemist. The three girls and Mr. Drew returned to the motel. After lunch he announced that he must leave.

"Good luck!" he said to the girls, then grinned. "By the time I talk with you again you'll have the mystery solved, I'm sure."

After Mr. Drew had left for River Heights,

Nancy suggested that she and the girls go to Mrs. Carrier's home and see how she was. They found her feeling better but rather weak.

"The doctor said I had a narrow escape," she told them.

"Is there any report from the lab about the poison?" Nancy queried.

Mrs. Carrier said she had not heard. Then she added, "I just can't understand Rawley. Why did he do such weird things? And I've been thinking about something else, too. I doubt that we'll find enough money and valuables in the house to pay all his debts."

Nancy told her about the other thousand-dollar bills the girls had discovered.

"Really?" the woman said. "I still have a strong hunch that Rawley didn't intend to return. He probably took everything he could carry, but didn't have time to clean off those bills."

Bess spoke up. "Couldn't Rawley's house be sold to pay his debts?"

"I doubt it," Mrs. Carrier answered. "Who would want to buy such a crazy-looking building?"

The girls did not reply because their answer would have been, "Nobody."

Seeing that Mrs. Carrier was tired, the girls said good-by to her and drove back to the motel.

"What shall we do now?" George asked.

Nancy replied, "I'd certainly like to find the skeleton's bracelet."

Bess asked, "Do you suppose Rawley himself wants it and doesn't dare go near his own house to get it?"

"I doubt that," Nancy replied. "If so, he would have stated in the note exactly where the bracelet is. I have a strong hunch another person wrote that message. But who?"

When the girls walked into the motel lobby, they noticed a letter in their mailbox. The clerk handed it to Nancy. She stared at it, puzzled.

"Where's the letter from?" Bess asked.

"Leupp, Arizona. The same place where your letter from Sleepy Deer was mailed."

"Hurry up and open it," George urged.

Nancy slit the envelope and took out a single sheet of paper. Typed on it was:

Find the Silver Armor Mask

The three girls stared at the unsigned message and Bess said, "I'll bet whoever wrote the note about the skeleton's bracelet sent this one too. It's in the same type."

George nodded. "And it could be Clyde Mead."

"How in the world did you figure that out?" Bess asked.

"It's easy," George answered. "Mead is involved with the Indian children and he has probably gone out there. He knows Nancy and I don't approve of him and he's playing these strange tricks on us. I think we should forget both anonymous messages."

Bess turned to Nancy. "Do you agree?"

Nancy took a few seconds to think before answering, then said, "To go even further, I now suspect that there may be some connection between Rawley Banister and Clyde Mead."

"What!" the cousins cried, and Bess asked, "Do you think Rawley is out in Leupp?"

"He could be," Nancy replied, "but more likely he's on his fast cruiser. Clyde Mead probably is working this Indian racket alone."

Bess was unconvinced, but George leaned toward Nancy's theory.

Nancy said, "As soon as Dad gets home, I'll phone him about this note. He may have some good advice."

At five o'clock she called her father. He was astounded to hear that the second mysterious note to Nancy had been mailed from Leupp, and that his daughter and George suspected Clyde Mead of having sent it.

"Nancy," he said, "I should attend to some business in Arizona. Suppose you and I make a quick trip out there and go to Leupp?"

"Oh, Dad," Nancy exclaimed, "that would be marvelous!"

Her father went on, "We can meet little

Sleepy Deer, if he exists, and get a line on Mead and perhaps Rawley."

Nancy was thrilled by her father's invitation and asked how soon they would start. He suggested that she come home at once.

"See if Bess's and George's parents will let them remain at the motel, so they can continue sleuthing in Mountainville until we get back."

"I'll ask them," Nancy replied. "If they can stay, shall I leave my car with them?"

"Yes. You can come home on the bus."

When Nancy told the girls about the Drews' plans, George said she would be glad to continue working on the case.

Bess looked a bit wistful. "I wish I could go to Arizona and see Sleepy Deer myself."

She also admitted to being a little afraid of carrying on the detective work without Nancy in charge.

Nancy smiled. "You've helped me solve so many mysteries, Bess, you could take over this one alone! Of course you girls are not to go to Rawley's house by yourselves. But perhaps Thomas will take you. Who knows, maybe by the time I get back, you will have found the skeleton's bracelet and the silver armor mask!"

"Do you think they're both in that weird house?" Bess queried.

"Yes," Nancy replied. "I feel the notes are genuine clues and not jokes."

The Marvins and Faynes gave permission for their daughters to remain at the motel but cautioned them to be careful. Nancy packed her clothes, had a quick dinner, then the girls drove her to the bus.

She arrived in River Heights about nine o'clock that evening. Hannah Gruen welcomed her with open arms.

"I'm glad you're safe," she said. "What adventures you've had!"

Nancy nodded, saying, "You were right about my getting into hot water, Hannah. I almost did!" She grinned impishly.

At the housekeeper's puzzled look, Nancy said, "Dad didn't tell you?"

She proceeded to explain about the disappearing bridge and the fire in the moat.

Mrs. Gruen sighed. "Now I'm doubly glad you're safe!"

Just then Mr. Drew came in and said he had obtained reservations on a jet going to Phoenix, Arizona. "From there, we'll take a connecting flight to Flagstaff, then go by helicopter to Leupp and look for little Sleepy Deer."

The next morning after attending Sunday church service, father and daughter returned to the house to pick up their luggage. Hannah wished them a good and a safe trip. Nancy blew kisses to her and Mr. Drew waved good-by as their taxi drove off to the airport. They had to change planes in New York City, and by late afternoon reached Phoenix.

"I guess we'd better stay here overnight," Mr. Drew said. "That will be just as well, because I want to make inquiries about the area where the Melody property was located. Also, we might find out something about Rawley Banister that will help us track him down."

The following morning the Drews went back to the airport and flew to Flagstaff. When they landed, the two immediately boarded a helicopter bound for the small town of Leupp.

The young pilot was pleasant and pointed out the interesting scenery along the way. There were mountains with mesas on top and extensive valleys, some as dry as deserts. Here and there flocks of sheep could be seen grazing.

"We don't have much rain in the summertime," the pilot said. "But fortunately sheep can live without water for long periods of time."

When he set the helicopter down just outside the village of Leupp, he said, "I'll return for you at four o'clock this afternoon."

The Drews walked up the main street of the Navaho town. The villagers stared at them but did not speak. The Indian men wore blue denim pants, bright shirts, scarves and large felt hats, with a band across their foreheads.

The women's clothing was more colorful. They wore multiple petticoats and velveteen blouses. Across an arm each woman carried a light blanket to be thrown around the shoulders when needed.

Nancy and her father went directly to the post office. "I hope the postmaster will give us Sleepy Deer's address," she whispered. "Sometimes postal authorities won't do this."

The Indian in charge proved to be an affable man. The Drews explained that they had come from the East and were looking for a child named Tom Sleepy Deer Smith.

"Could you tell us where he lives?" Nancy asked.

The answer was a bit disconcerting. "The little boy you mean lives several miles outside of Leupp."

Nancy's heart sank. How were she and her father to get there? Suddenly she had an idea and asked, "Would it be possible for us to rent horses?"

The postmaster inquired, "Can you use a western saddle?"

"Oh yes," she replied. "I've ridden in the West before."

The man gave the Drews directions to a hogan at the edge of town. It was a typical mud-covered log hut. The elderly couple who lived there were glad to rent two horses. They suggested that Nancy ride the horse named Black Feet.

The husband gave directions to the small

Indian village where Sleepy Deer lived. Mr. Drew and Nancy set off at a canter along a narrow road, but soon found it was easier and more comfortable to ride on the sun-baked grass. It took them two hours to reach the other village. Here the hogans were scattered along the base of a craggy cliff.

The dusty riders stopped in front of a trading post with blankets, hats, jewelry, and groceries for sale. They dismounted and tied their horses. Mr. Drew went inside to inquire where they could find Tom Sleepy Deer Smith.

"Last house," the man said, pointing toward the east. Mr. Drew thanked him and came outside. He and Nancy started walking toward the Smith home. Within minutes Navahos poured from the various dwellings and followed the two up the street. Apparently someone had spread the word that visitors were in the village.

When they reached the last house, a man and a little boy came outside. The Drews said how-do-you-do, and Nancy smiled warmly at the child.

"Is your name Tom Sleepy Deer Smith?" she asked.

"Yes," the little boy said shyly.

"We've ridden a good many miles to see you," Nancy told him.

Mr. Drew spoke to the father about the Navaho territory and said he understood that certain people were making claims on property which belonged to the reservation.

"We have a little trouble," the man answered.

Nancy leaned over and said to Sleepy Deer, "We wanted to tell you that our friend Bess Marvin loved your letter."

The little boy looked at his father but did not reply.

Nancy continued, "You did receive the money she sent you, didn't you?"

Again Sleepy Deer looked at his father but said nothing, and the Drews realized the Smiths had become suspicious of them.

"Don't be afraid to talk," Mr. Drew said. "My daughter and I are not government investigators. This is just a friendly call."

Still the Smiths did not reply. Before Nancy had a chance to ask another question, they all heard a warning shout. Looking in the direction from which it had come, Nancy's heart pounded. Her horse had broken loose and was running wildly up the street toward them! The villagers scattered and Mr. Drew moved out of the way.

Nancy stood still. Spreading her arms sideways to full length, she yelled, "Whoa, Black Feet! Whoa!"

CHAPTER XVII

Indian Powwow

NANCY made a flying leap and caught the horse's bridle. "Whoa! Black Feet, whoa!" she cried out. "Nobody's going to hurt you."

The frightened animal seemed to recognize her and knew she was kind. He came to a dead stop that almost threw Nancy to the roadway. But she hung on, pulled down the horse's head, and began to pat him. Within seconds he was as docile as he had been while she was riding him.

Sleepy Deer began to clap and exclaimed, "You are brave girl!"

The Navahos looked at Nancy admiringly and chanted a little song. Mr. Smith said it was a song of thanksgiving and praise because Nancy had been in grave danger and had acted courageously. She had kept some of the villagers from being injured by the runaway horse.

Mr. Drew clasped his daughter tightly in his arms and said, "You took your life in your hands, my dear, but I'm very proud of you."

The crowd melted away. As Nancy once more tied Black Feet to a post—securely this time—Mr. Smith said eagerly, "Now I tell you the whole story."

He revealed that his son had not received any money and two other children in the village had been asked the same question by tourists.

"They get no money from anybody either," he added.

The man went on to say that the people in the village were poor. Due to a very severe winter and a hot, dry summer, their crop of corn had been sparse.

Sleepy Deer spoke up. "Maybe we have a rain dance soon, so that Rain God send rain to make the corn grow."

The Drews looked at each other. There was no question but that these people needed help.

Sleepy Deer's father continued to tell his story. About two years ago, two men had come to the Indian village.

"We think they are just tourists," Mr. Smith said.

He revealed it was sometime later that the Navahos became suspicious. During a powwow they learned that the two visitors had been writing down the names of all the villagers, particularly those of the children.

"Then one day another tourist ask a boy if he write letter to someone in a distant place. Answer is no. We Navahos worried something is wrong."

"You didn't report it to the authorities?" Nancy asked.

Sleepy Deer and his father shook their heads. Mr. Smith said, "We afraid of trouble by those men, so we keep quiet."

Mr. Drew told him that since the villagers were innocent of any wrongdoing, there was nothing to fear.

"And the two men should be reported and arrested," he added.

Nancy asked if the two inquisitive strangers had given their names.

Mr. Smith nodded. "They say their names are Fitch and Rawley."

The Drews were excited to hear this. They felt sure that Rawley was Rawley Banister and that Fitch was Clyde Mead! Furthermore, this seemed like definite proof that the two men were pals and had been working rackets together for some time.

Nancy asked, "Did Mr. Fitch or Mr. Rawley ever return to your village?"

"No," Mr. Smith replied.

This set Nancy to thinking. If neither of the men had been in the area recently, who had mailed the fake letters? She asked Mr. Smith if he knew.

He said that everyone in the village had been questioned and all had denied any knowledge of this. The Indians in Leupp had also been consulted and nobody there knew anything about the mailing of the letters.

"Then it must have been done by a tourist," Mr. Drew said. He turned to Mr. Smith. "Do any of the tourists come here often—I mean, the same tourist?"

"No."

Sleepy Deer's father said a bus carrying sightseers came twice a week to Leupp and brought visitors to his village.

"Later today one come here," he added.

"Then we'll wait and talk to the people on it," Mr. Drew told him.

Just then Mrs. Smith came from the family's hogan. She spoke to her husband in their native language.

He smiled and said to the Drews in English, "Would you accept an invitation to eat with us?"

Nancy and her father smiled also.

"We'd be delighted to," Mr. Drew answered.

Their host led the way into the hogan. The walls were whitewashed and on them hung a bow and arrow, several pieces of very fine colorful embroidery, a grotesque mask, and a small shelf with a few books.

There were no chairs in the room. The floor was covered with bright-colored linoleum. In the center of it were several bowls of food.

The Smith family sat down in a semicircle and motioned for Nancy and her father to squat also. The meal consisted of bean sprouts, pieces of mutton cooked with hominy, and corn pudding. One large flat saucer contained several layers of paper-thin corn bread.

"This is delicious," Nancy told her host and hostess. To Sleepy Deer's mother she added, "You are a very good cook."

The Smiths smiled and nodded but made no response. Nancy had once read that many Indians are embarrassed by compliments.

Nancy said, "Would you be willing to let me and some of my friends help Sleepy Deer and the other children in your village?"

She expected a quick affirmative response and was shocked to see dark looks come over the Smiths' faces.

"Oh dear!" she thought. "I've said something wrong."

Her father, however, guessed what was going through the Smiths' minds. What proof did they have that the Drews would not use the Indians for some ulterior motive of their own as Fitch and Rawley had?

Mr. Drew explained he was a lawyer and his daughter liked to solve mysteries. He said they probably knew who the swindlers were and that two of their friends had already given money for the Navaho children to one of the men.

"We're trying to find both swindlers," Mr. Drew said. "That's why we came here."

Finally he convinced the Smiths of the Drews' sincerity. Nancy and her father thanked them for their hospitality. Then Nancy asked Sleepy Deer if he would please show them around the village. Together they climbed up some natural stone steps to the top of the cliff.

While the Drews were enjoying a view of the surrounding countryside, the little boy said, "Long ago when the white man come to take our land, we Navahos move up here."

Nancy recalled having heard that when the western territory of the United States was being settled, soldiers greatly outnumbered the Indians. To avoid being taken prisoner or killed, the Indians had fled to the flat tops of the mountains. When peace was restored, they had returned to the valleys.

"Now we go to see the bus," Sleepy Deer said as the three climbed down.

He led the Drews up the main street of the village and waited. About twenty minutes later the bus arrived. Nancy and her father carefully watched the tourists who disembarked. Most of them were women and none of them looked shifty-eyed or suspicious.

The driver and the guide stayed in the bus while the passengers looked at the various articles which the Indians had brought out to sell.

"I'll talk to the driver," Mr. Drew said. "Maybe he can give us a clue to those swindlers. Nancy, why don't you speak to the guide?"

As Mr. Drew was about to climb into the bus, the guide stepped out. Nancy approached him. "May I ask you a few questions?" she said.

The man looked annoyed and answered, "You're not paying for this tour. But okay, go ahead. What do you want to know?"

Nancy was not sure how to proceed with this unpleasant person, but she smiled and said, "You'll be surprised to hear this, but my father and I are out here tracking down a couple of swindlers."

"What!" the guide exclaimed.

Nancy decided to tell the full story. When she finished, a puzzled look came over the man's face.

"You know," he said, "I may be involved in this swindle—entirely innocently, I assure you."

"I believe you," Nancy remarked, eager for the man to explain further.

The guide said that about eighteen months

ago, two men who had been passengers on the same bus trip had asked him if he would like to earn a little extra money.

"I said sure, and they told me they'd write to me once in a while and enclose letters which I was to mail in the Leupp post office. I didn't see any harm in that and each time they sent a letter for me to mail they enclosed two dollars."

"What were the names of these men?" Nancy asked.

"Fitch and Rawley. But the envelopes that came to me and the letters to be mailed did not have the sender's name or address."

"Where had they been mailed from?" the young detective asked.

The guide said they had come from many different places. "I never paid attention to the names on the envelopes I was to mail or where they were going, so I can't tell you anything about that."

On a sudden inspiration Nancy asked, "By any chance do you happen to have with you one of the letters to be mailed?"

"Yes I do," the guide replied.

He took an envelope from his pocket and handed it to Nancy, then hurried off to his group of tourists.

Nancy gasped. The letter was addressed to Mrs. Carrier!

At this moment Mr. Drew stepped from the bus and reported that he had learned nothing from the driver.

"But I learned plenty!" Nancy told him. "Look at this!"

Her father stared at the envelope in disbelief. Then he suggested that Nancy open it.

Inside was a note in the same childish handwriting as the one Bess had received. The letter contained a similar message and the signature was Mary Singing Brook Dare.

"This is great evidence!" Mr. Drew remarked.

Nancy wondered if Singing Brook lived here or in Leupp. She hurried off to find Sleepy Deer.

He said Mary was a playmate of his. "I take you to see her," the boy offered.

As Nancy suspected, little Singing Brook had never heard of Mrs. Carrier and had received no money from her.

Mr. Drew looked grim as he said, "Those swindlers may be working their racket in other reservations. I will notify the Department of the Interior as soon as we get back to the hotel."

As the Drews walked toward their horses, they saw the driver summoning them. Hurrying forward, Nancy asked, "What's up?"

"Listen to this radio report!" the man said excitedly.

The announcer was saying that news of a new copper deposit had just flashed over the teletype.

Already people were rushing to the area to put in claims for the surrounding land.

"It's turning into a riot!" the announcer finished.

Nancy and her father looked at each other. Mr. Drew exclaimed, "Nancy, that's near the property that the swindler sold the Melodys, and it's only six miles from here!"

"Let's go!" Nancy cried out and ran toward her horse.

CHAPTER XVIII

Bridge Out!

THE two horses sensed that their riders were in a hurry. They galloped hard across the dry valley dotted with cacti. Presently Nancy and her father saw a sign.

"This is the end of the reservation," Mr. Drew remarked. "We don't have much farther to go."

As they neared the site of the copper discovery, the Drews saw a crowd of people milling around. They had come in cars, by helicopter and on horseback. Men were shouting loudly and arguing angrily.

"I spoke for this piece first!" one man cried.

"You didn't! It's mine!" said another.

Nancy and her father halted at the fringe of the crowd and dismounted. In this barren area there was not even a tree to which they could tie the horses.

"Now, Black Feet, don't you dare run away," Nancy admonished the horse.

She and her father strode forward. Claims were being made by miners, real-estate men, and others hoping to make a quick fortune. A mannish-looking woman was haranguing the crowd, urging them to leave.

"This land-boom deal must be settled peacefully," she shouted. No one paid any attention.

As the Drews came closer, they realized that the woman was standing up in the stirrups of her saddle so she could be heard.

Mr. Drew chuckled softly and said to Nancy, "That woman has the right idea. I think I'll try to help her."

He pushed his way among the fist-waving group and spoke to her. She smiled at him and said, "Come on!"

Mr. Drew swung himself up lightly in back of her. He clapped his hands loudly and asked for the crowd's attention.

Seeing this, Nancy began clapping also and yelling, "Quiet, everybody! Quiet!"

The two commanding voices silenced the crowd. Mr. Drew said in a loud voice:

"I represent a client who received a deed to property near here. The deal turned out to be a fraud. What proof have you people that the report of a copper deposit may not have been given out by swindlers?"

His listeners looked at one another and began murmuring. Mr. Drew went on, "Surely someone has title to this property. Why don't you find out who it is instead of trying to stake a claim? My advice to you is to leave before somebody gets hurt. If the man who has made the highest bid will give his name and address to me, I promise to put the owner in touch with him."

A grizzled, middle-aged man, with a deep suntan and bright blue, honest-looking eyes, stepped forward. "Thank you," he said and wrote his name and address on a piece of paper.

Rather grudgingly the crowd dispersed. Nancy was smiling broadly. She was so proud of her father!

The woman on the horse said to him, "I don't know how you did it. Many of the men around here are a pretty tough lot! I came because I think this land belongs to my family."

Mr. Drew smiled and told the woman he thought she had a lot of courage. Then he rode off with Nancy.

"It's getting late," he said. "I hope our pilot doesn't take off without us."

A strong breeze had come up and Nancy was fascinated watching the huge balls of tumbleweed rolling across the plain. The Drews made good time to Leupp and to their relief found the helicopter waiting. They returned the horses, paid the owners for their use, and said good-by.

By the time Nancy and her father reached their hotel in Phoenix, it was past eight o'clock. "I'm famished," said Nancy.

While they were enjoying a steak dinner, Mr. Drew remarked, "Nancy, do you mind returning to River Heights alone? I have more business to attend to out here, and I'm sure you're eager to get back to Mountainville and report what you've learned."

"I certainly am." Nancy's eyes danced in anticipation.

A little later she got in touch with the airline and made reservations for an early-morning flight to New York, then one to River Heights.

Immediately after breakfast the next day Mr. Drew went with Nancy to the airport and wished her a good trip.

"I haven't forgotten about notifying the Department of the Interior," he said. "I'll do so first thing."

Nancy waved to him as she stepped through the cabin doorway of the plane. Hours later she reached River Heights and took a taxi home.

Hannah Gruen hugged and kissed the young detective. "Oh, Nancy, I'm so glad to see you. And how is your dad?"

"He's fine but busy. Wait until I tell you the news!"

During supper she gave Hannah all the exciting details of her western adventure. The housekeeper's eyes opened wide in astonishment. "So you have proof that Clyde Mead is a swindler!" she exclaimed.

They had just finished eating when Ned Nickerson telephoned. "I'm glad I found you at home," he said. "I understand from Bess and George that you and your dad took off in a big hurry for Arizona."

Nancy promised to tell him about it the next time she saw him.

Ned chuckled. "That's going to be sooner than you think. Burt and Dave and I are free tomorrow. We thought we'd go to Mountainville and help on the mystery. That is, if you haven't already solved it."

"Only part of it," Nancy replied, but refused to divulge any more on the phone.

"Okay," the young man answered. Then he asked teasingly, "How about your letting us boys clear up the rest of it?"

"I dare you!" she answered.

Ned laughed. "We'll pick you up at ten o'clock. One of the boys will call Bess and George and tell them to expect us."

Before going to bed, Nancy unpacked the clothes she had used for her trip and substituted appropriate ones for Mountainville. The next morning she said good-by to Hannah and drove off in Ned's car. Burt and Dave were with him.

They arrived at twelve o'clock and checked

into the Ruppert Motel. Bess and George were waiting and said they had reserved a table in the dining room.

As soon as they sat down, Bess said, "I want to hear all about everything. Who wants the floor first?"

"I do," Dave replied. "We checked on Clyde Mead's claim that he was a professor at Emerson. He was there only three months giving special lectures on marine biology. He wasn't very well liked and suddenly quit."

"That sounds like him," George remarked. "He probably had another racket coming up."

Bess looked hurt. "You could be wrong, George. Well, Nancy, begin your story."

"Before I start," Nancy said, "tell me, how is Mrs. Carrier?"

"She's fine," Bess replied. "By the way, the poison on that portrait is aconite."

George spoke up. "We drove over to see Mrs. Carrier this morning and got the key to Rawley's place."

As Nancy told what she and her father had discovered in Arizona, her listeners were spellbound. But Bess looked downcast.

"Poor little Sleepy Deer!" she said.

All the young people vowed to help the Navaho children of Leupp and the nearby community where Sleepy Deer lived. They appointed Bess to be chairman of the committee.

After lunch Nancy and her friends decided to drive to Rawley Banister's house. She and Ned started off in her car. The others followed in his. The convertible reached the top of the hill first. The guard's car was there. Ned parked and they started across the bridge just as the others arrived.

Without warning the moat flamed up! Nancy and Ned hurried to get across.

"I'm glad we didn't have to put down the saplings," Ned remarked.

By this time Nancy was about halfway over, with Ned at her heels. Suddenly she felt the bridge sag. Before she could warn Ned to retreat, the half of the structure on which they were walking parted from the other half and began to plunge downward.

On shore Bess screamed as Nancy and Ned started to slide toward the flaming water.

"Oh no!" George cried out, horrified.

Realizing their danger, Nancy and Ned acted fast. He dropped down, grabbed the wide steel beam, and held on with all his strength. Nancy managed to clasp one of his ankles with both hands. For a couple of seconds Nancy hung in mid-air, then she swung one leg over the bridge and wrapped the other around the swaying support.

"We must save them!" Bess cried out.

Nancy hung in mid-air

Burt said, "We'll make a human chain!" He examined the section where the bridge was sagging from the shore and found that an exceedingly strong hinge was attached to an upright hidden in the embankment.

He offered to be anchor man and lay down on the ground, his toes tucked firmly through the bumper of Ned's car. Dave stretched out on the bridge with Burt holding his ankles. George crawled beyond the boys and Dave grabbed her ankles, but she could not quite reach Ned's outstretched arms.

"Bess, you'll have to help me," she said.

The situation was so desperate that Bess had no chance to think of being afraid. She took her place, with her ankles tightly anchored by George. Ned could reach her easily. The human chain was ready.

"All set!" Burt called.

Slowly Nancy pulled herself up and crawled to safety across the bodies of her friends. Ned came next. Then Burt and Dave assisted George and Bess to their feet. The exhausted young people flopped onto the ground. It was several minutes before anyone spoke.

Finally Dave broke the silence. "Well, I guess it's back to the saplings for us!"

Ned got up and examined the hinge of the bridge. "Now we know how this thing appears and disappears. Evidently some mechanism divides it in the middle, then the two halves part and drop below the water."

Bess had not recovered from her fright. "I don't want to cross that burning water on the saplings," she stated firmly.

"Then I guess you'll have to stay on this side alone," George told her.

By the time the boys had the saplings in place, Bess had changed her mind and the group went across.

"I wonder where the guard is," said Nancy, and called out loudly, "Anyone here?" There was no reply.

"That's strange," Ned remarked. He too called loudly but received no answer.

Nancy suspected that something might have happened to the man and suggested they start a search for him. They found the guard lying unconscious in back of the house.

"He's been attacked!" George exclaimed.

Bess was afraid that the guard's assailant might be inside the house. "Do you think we really should go in?" she asked.

Ned was already kneeling on the ground and giving the guard first-aid. A minute later the man opened his eyes and looked around blankly.

"You're all right," Ned told him. "Did someone knock you out?"

"Yes," the guard said as Ned helped him to stand up. "A masked man rushed at me from around the corner of the house and hit me on the head. Before I blacked out, I saw him throw a lighted taper match into the moat. I think he would have dropped me in, but he heard a car coming and ran across the bridge. Then I lost consciousness."

"What did he look like?" Nancy queried.

"Tall and slender. Dark hair."

The young people concluded that the fugitive had tampered with the bridge before disappearing into the woods.

Bess dramatically told the guard what had happened and added, "He's an evil man."

Burt smiled. "That's putting it mildly."

As the young people entered the hall, George asked, "Where would one look for a silver armor mask?"

Dave replied, "On a silver knight."

Nancy snapped her fingers and said excitedly, "I have it! The robot! He's silver in color, and his face is like a mask."

"Okay, so it is," George remarked. "But what does that prove?"

Everyone waited tensely for Nancy's answer. "Maybe," she said, "if we insert a certain tape, we'll learn some secret!"

"But which tape?" Bess questioned. "You might put one in that would blow us all sky-high!"

Nancy said they would look over all of them

and see if they could find an identifying mark indicating the right one. The group went to the kitchen and she opened the drawer which held the tapes. Carefully they examined them one by one.

Finally Ned held up a reel. "I think this might be it," he said. "It's marked *Top Secret.*"

CHAPTER XIX

Poison!

NANCY rolled the robot from the closet and inserted the *Top Secret* tape. As the whirring sound began, she warned everyone to stand back.

She and her friends waited with pounding hearts to see what he would do. The whirring became louder. Then suddenly the mechanical man was propelled through the swinging door and out to the hallway. He stopped at the foot of the stairs, jerkily raised his right arm, and pointed upward.

Ned asked, "Does he mean there's something on the second floor we should investigate?"

"I'll bet you're right," George answered. "Let's go up there and see what we can find!"

She climbed the stairs with Burt. Bess and Dave followed.

Nancy said to Ned, "Let's stay down here and see what else the robot does."

He nodded and the two stood at one side of the hall to watch him.

"Robby's moving!" Nancy whispered.

The mechanical man turned abruptly, rolled across the hall, and went into the den. Nancy and Ned trailed him.

"That's interesting," he remarked, watching intently.

The robot had stopped in front of Rawley's desk. Now he raised his right arm and pointed to a certain drawer.

"I think he wants someone to open it," Nancy said.

Ned offered to and walked forward. He tried to pull out the drawer but found it locked.

"What am I supposed to do now?" Ned asked. "This creature is programmed to be as mysterious as his owner."

A moment later the mechanical man began waving his right arm in a circle. Nancy and Ned looked at each other, puzzled. What did this gesture mean?

Nancy made a guess. "Maybe Robby is indicating that we are to rotate something."

"Perhaps it's the knob," Ned said.

He turned the knob until it came off. "Now what?" he asked. "Even if this has unlocked the drawer, there's still no way to pull it out. Any ideas, Nancy?"

"No."

The couple stood looking at the desk for several seconds. Then both of them leaned down and began working on the edges of the drawer with their fingernails.

"It's moving!" Nancy exclaimed.

Seconds later they were able to pull out the drawer. It contained a neat pile of papers. On the top was a folded document marked: *The Last Will and Testament of Rawley Banister.*

"I'm sure we're not supposed to read this," Nancy stated.

Ned closed the drawer and screwed the knob back on.

Nancy said, "I'll tell Mrs. Carrier and Thomas about the will as soon as we see them."

When the desk was locked, the robot turned and rolled away. They followed him back into the hall. The mechanical man stopped directly under the Oriental wall hanging and pointed upward.

"There certainly must be a secret in this picture," Ned remarked.

Nancy nodded. "It may have something to do with the will."

Suddenly the robot turned and began to move forward. They walked after him, but apparently the tape was almost finished. He went to the kitchen and the whirring sound stopped.

Nancy removed the tape and locked Robby in the closet. She and Ned returned to the front hall.

Bess called excitedly from upstairs, "Here comes Mr. Mead! Don't let him in!"

George, Burt, and Dave appeared at the head of the stairs.

"Yes, it's Clyde Mead," George confirmed. "But I think we should let him in. If we don't, how are we going to capture that swindler?"

"You're right," Ned called up. "The instant he comes to this door, we'll tackle him!"

George said, "I'll be right down to help you. But not by the stairs. Every time I've been in this house, I've wanted to ride on the crooked banister. Now I'm going to do it!"

"I'll go too!" Burt said. "Let me get on first. You follow."

"All right," George agreed.

They climbed up. Burt had chosen the banister which had been sawed off at the wall. Nancy was about to suggest they switch to the other railing, but it was too late. George and Burt had started down. Their twisting descent was so swift they were almost swung off.

"It's like riding a roller coaster!" George cried.

As they neared the bottom, both she and Burt grabbed the rail hard and tried to stop. But they were not able to. The next moment there was a loud crash. A gaping hole appeared in the plasterboard wall and George and Burt disappeared through it.

"Oh!" screamed Bess, who was halfway down the stairway.

Nancy and Ned rushed to the opening and looked inside. George and Burt were just picking themselves up from the floor.

"Are you hurt?" Nancy asked quickly.

Before George and Burt could answer, a solemn voice announced hollowly, "Now you cannot escape! You're trapped among the poisons!"

The dire message was repeated.

CHAPTER XX

The Capture

DURING the excitement which followed George and Burt's crash through the wall into the poison room, loud thumping could be heard on the front door. The other young people intent on trying to help the couple step out paid no attention.

"Are you all right?" Nancy asked, leaning through the opening.

"We're fine as far as we can see," George replied, "but I'd like to find out what's here. Hand me a flashlight, will you?"

Ned produced one from his pocket and gave it to her. A strange sight met their eyes! There were rows of shelves, each filled with metal boxes alongside bottles marked POISON. Fortunately, none of the bottles had been overturned or broken, so their contents had not spilled onto George and Burt.

"I guess Rawley Banister had a mania for poisons," George remarked. "On some of these bottles are the names of the poisons from the plants and reptiles that the serpents in the Oriental wall hanging are eating."

Burt added, "Here's the tape recorder that greeted us with that fiendish message."

The thumping on the front door became more insistent. Bess turned to Nancy. "What shall we do? I'm sure that's Mr. Mead."

As Nancy hesitated to let him in, Ned suggested that Burt hand out one of the metal boxes so he could see what was inside. Ned set it on a step of the stairway and opened the lid. The box was filled with money!

Nancy was hardly paying attention. She was thinking, "If we let Mr. Mead go we may never have a chance to capture him. But if we open the door, he'll see what's here and I don't think that's a good idea. He might have a gun and help himself to this treasure."

She turned to Ned and relayed her thoughts to him. "Suppose I ask Mead to come around to the back door? You and Dave can let him in."

"And make him a prisoner!" Ned answered. "Come on, Dave!"

Nancy hurried to the front door and asked, "Who's there?"

"Clyde Mead. You're Nancy Drew, I guess.

You told me about this interesting place and I thought I'd come to see it."

"All right," Nancy answered in as calm a voice as she could manage. "Please go around to the rear door."

"Right away," the man said affably.

For a second Nancy felt sorry for him, knowing what was going to happen, but she brushed the thought aside. The man was a swindler and should be handed over to the police.

Meanwhile Ned and Dave had hurried to the rear door in the kitchen. When the man opened it, the two husky football players tackled him.

"What's the meaning of this?" Mead cried out angrily as the boys helped him up but held his arms tightly.

"You'll find out in a few minutes," Ned told him.

The prisoner struggled to free himself. "Let me go! I haven't done anything!" he shouted. "If it's my money you want, take it but get your hands off me!"

Mead was not a muscular man and Dave had no trouble holding him alone.

"Ned, get the others," Dave directed. Mead looked at him questioningly but received no explanation.

When Ned reached the hall he was astounded to see the lower steps of the crooked stairway piled with small metal boxes. Each was open and every one contained money.

"There are thousands of dollars here," Nancy told him. "Probably enough to pay all the people Rawley swindled, and lots left over."

"Here's a list of his victims," George interposed.

"And we found the skeleton's bracelet!" exclaimed Bess, holding it up. "It's even more gorgeous than in the photograph we saw in Rawley's book."

The rubies in the serpents' eyes gleamed brightly and Ned saw that the gold jewel piece was studded with turquoise.

"I wonder where Rawley got the bracelet?" he asked. "I'll bet he bought it from the thief who stole it in Mexico."

"Probably," Nancy agreed. "Here's a tag that says it came from the arm of an ancient Aztec woman's skeleton."

She led the way to the kitchen. When Mead saw the whole group, he paled.

Bess was the first to speak. "You are a faker, Mr. Clyde Mead. You took my money for a little Navaho boy but never gave it to him!"

"What do you mean?" the man asked. "Of course I did."

Nancy told about the trip she and her father had made to Arizona and what they had learned. Mead suddenly lost all his bravado.

"Okay," he said. "I was pressed for money and thought up that scheme of getting some. I'll repay everybody whose cash I took."

George spoke up. "We found a printing press in the basement. Did you use it to make your fake pamphlets about the Indians?"

"Yes."

Nancy looked straight at the man and said, "You weren't alone in that scheme and in a whole lot of others, too. You're a pal of Rawley Banister's and the two of you swindled a number of people."

Mead's jaw dropped. He stared at Nancy as if he could not believe his ears. Convinced that the young detective had concrete evidence to prove her charges, Mead made a complete confession.

"Where's Rawley now?" Nancy asked him.

"You figure it out. He left here saying he was going on a long trip. Rawley owed me a great deal of money for helping him with his schemes.

"When I reminded him of this, he said half-jokingly, 'I'll give you two hints. If you can find the answers in my house to two riddles, you can have whatever you locate.' "

Mead said that one clue was, "Find the skeleton's bracelet." The other was, "Find the silver armor mask."

"I had no idea what Rawley meant, but I asked him for a key. He gave me one to the rear door of this crazy house. The first time I was here someone came to the front door and banged the knocker loudly. "Whoever it was seemed very angry," Mead said. "Almost simultaneously a recorded message told the person to come back some other time.

"When he was gone, I traced the 'voice' to a miniature tape recorder cleverly hidden over the door and tore it out. I knew I'd be coming here again and didn't want any visitors to plan on returning."

Mead mopped his forehead with a handkerchief as he continued, "I kept out of the way of the man who worked for Rawley. But I met him once. He was the general handyman and incidentally he knew how to make the bridge go up and down. Also he sometimes set the moat on fire. His name is Mickey Garver."

"He must have been the one who knocked out the guard," Nancy remarked.

Mead said he did not know about that, but Garver had told him he had set the motel fires and stolen the Melodys' papers to protect Rawley from being prosecuted for that swindle.

"Who telephoned me and tried to get my father off the case?" Nancy questioned.

"That was Rawley. I found out Mr. Drew had come to Mountainville to work on the case. When you and your father learned that Rawley had jumped bail, you started to track him down. When he called me from New York City, I told him what you two were up to. Rawley said he was going to get the Drews off the case at once."

Bess spoke up. "But he didn't!"

Nancy said to Mead, "I suppose you sent the notes to me about the bracelet and the mask. When you couldn't find them yourself, you wanted me to do it, then you would try to steal them."

The prisoner admitted this was true, saying he had kept a close scrutiny on the girls' activities in Mountainville.

George grinned. "We figured out the riddle of the mask, then found the bracelet."

Mead looked at the young people unbelievingly. "I thought you were smart enough to decipher the messages, but had doubts that you were smart enough to find the bracelet." He sighed in disgust. "If I hadn't taken money from Bess Marvin and Rawley's sister for the Indian children, I never would have been caught," he added ruefully.

Ned told the man he was not so sure of this. "The police are delving into Rawley's affairs and will discover that you two were working together."

Suddenly the prisoner cried out, "You'll never get Rawley! He's dead!"

Everyone in the kitchen gasped. "What do you mean?" Burt asked.

"A few days ago I saw a newspaper report that

his cruiser blew up and he drowned. Rawley was using an assumed name that only I knew. I saw the item about the accidental death of De Koork Retsinab. Substituting the letter 'c' for the last 'k' in De Koork, you will find that this man's name spelled backward is Crooked Banister."

"And you didn't report this to the police authorities?" Dave asked Mead.

"No. I was afraid of being found out."

Ned asked Mead if he knew about the robot.

"Yes. Rawley told me the sound of a voice activated it."

Nancy mentioned that she and her friends had found portraits with the faces painted out and poison put on them. "Have you any idea why?" she asked.

Mead thought a moment. "Rawley once said to me, 'I hate all my relatives except my parents and brother and sister. I'd like to poison them all!' I liked Rawley but he was kind of wacky."

The questioning was interrupted by the rapping of the front-door knocker. Nancy and Ned went to see who was there. The callers proved to be Mrs. Carrier, Thomas Banister, and three policemen.

"Is Clyde Mead here?" one of the officers asked.

"Yes," Ned replied. "He's our prisoner in the kitchen."

"Good," said the officer. "The authorities finally trailed Mead to Mountainville."

Nancy told him that Mead had confessed and implicated Mickey Garver. The officer said the handyman would be taken into custody.

Nancy led the way to the kitchen. Within seconds Mead was being escorted out the back door by the three officers.

"Didn't I see a hole in the hallway wall?" Mrs. Carrier asked, a puzzled look on her face. "And boxes on the stairway?"

Nancy quickly related all that had happened. Then the other young people showed her and Thomas the money, the skeleton's bracelet, and the bottles of poison.

When the excitement over the tremendous find had died down, Nancy told Mrs. Carrier and her brother of Rawley's death.

His sister said soberly, "I believe Rawley had a premonition of his death. That's why he left the message and key with me."

Thomas nodded solemnly. "I'm glad Rawley will be spared having earthly authorities punish him."

Then he added, "One thing is not clear to me. How did Rawley get into the space back of the bookcase without breaking the wall?"

Nancy said they had not figured this out yet. "Perhaps the robot can tell us. By the way, he showed us where Rawley's will is."

"We'll look at that later," Thomas said.

The group returned to the kitchen and examined the unused tapes. One was marked BC.

"Maybe this means bookcase," Nancy said.

"Try it," Mrs. Carrier directed.

The robot was brought from the closet and the tape inserted. Everyone watched him intently. The whirring sound started and the mechanical man rolled out to the hall, then into the living room. He stopped in front of the bookcase.

Then the robot raised his arms high over his head and pointed to the top of the bookcase. Next he moved his arms as if indicating that the piece of furniture was to be pulled out. At this gesture the tape ended.

"I'll take a look," Ned said and swung to Dave's shoulders.

Leaning forward he gave the bookcase a tug and it moved toward him easily. When Dave and Ned rolled it out into the room, the searchers found a door leading into the narrow poison room.

"This must have been the original door into the hall," Burt remarked.

The bookcase was shoved back into place and the watchers heard a click.

Mrs. Carrier turned toward Nancy and her friends. "How can we ever repay you for all you've done?" she said.

"We want no reward," Nancy said quickly. "It has been a great pleasure to meet you people and work on the mystery."

The young detective looked dreamily into space, wondering what her next case would be. It soon followed and became known as *The Secret of Mirror Bay*.

Thomas Banister spoke up. "You girls have brought to a close one of the most baffling mysteries I have ever heard of. We can never thank you enough. Nancy Drew, you're a wonder!"

Nancy smiled and laid a hand on the mechanical man. "Do you know who really solved this mystery?" she asked. "Robby!"